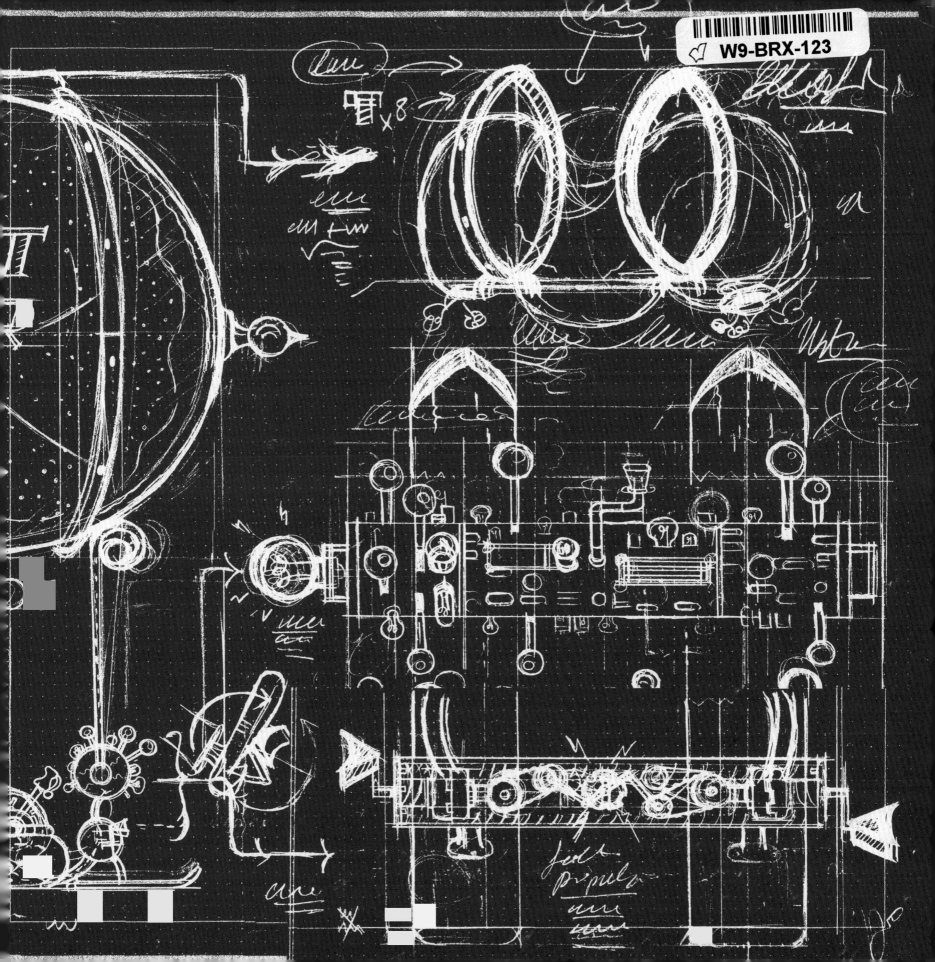

Dedicated to Isa

Special thanks to Alex Spiro,
Alberto Guitián, David Rubín, Jorge Peral,
Roque Romero, Miguel Robledo,
Alex Reverdin and my brother Nacho.

MIX
Paper from responsible sources
FSC® C101807

Pablo & Jane and the Hot Air Contraption © Flying Eye Books 2015.

This is a first edition published in 2015 by Flying Eye Books,
an imprint of Nobrow Ltd. 62 Great Eastern Street, London, EC2A 3QR.

Published in the US by Nobrow (US) Inc.

ISBN: 978-1-909263-36-9

Order from www.flyingeyebooks.com

JOSÉ DOMINGO

PABLO & JANE

AND THE HOT AIR CONTRAPTION

FLYING EYE BOOKS
London – New York

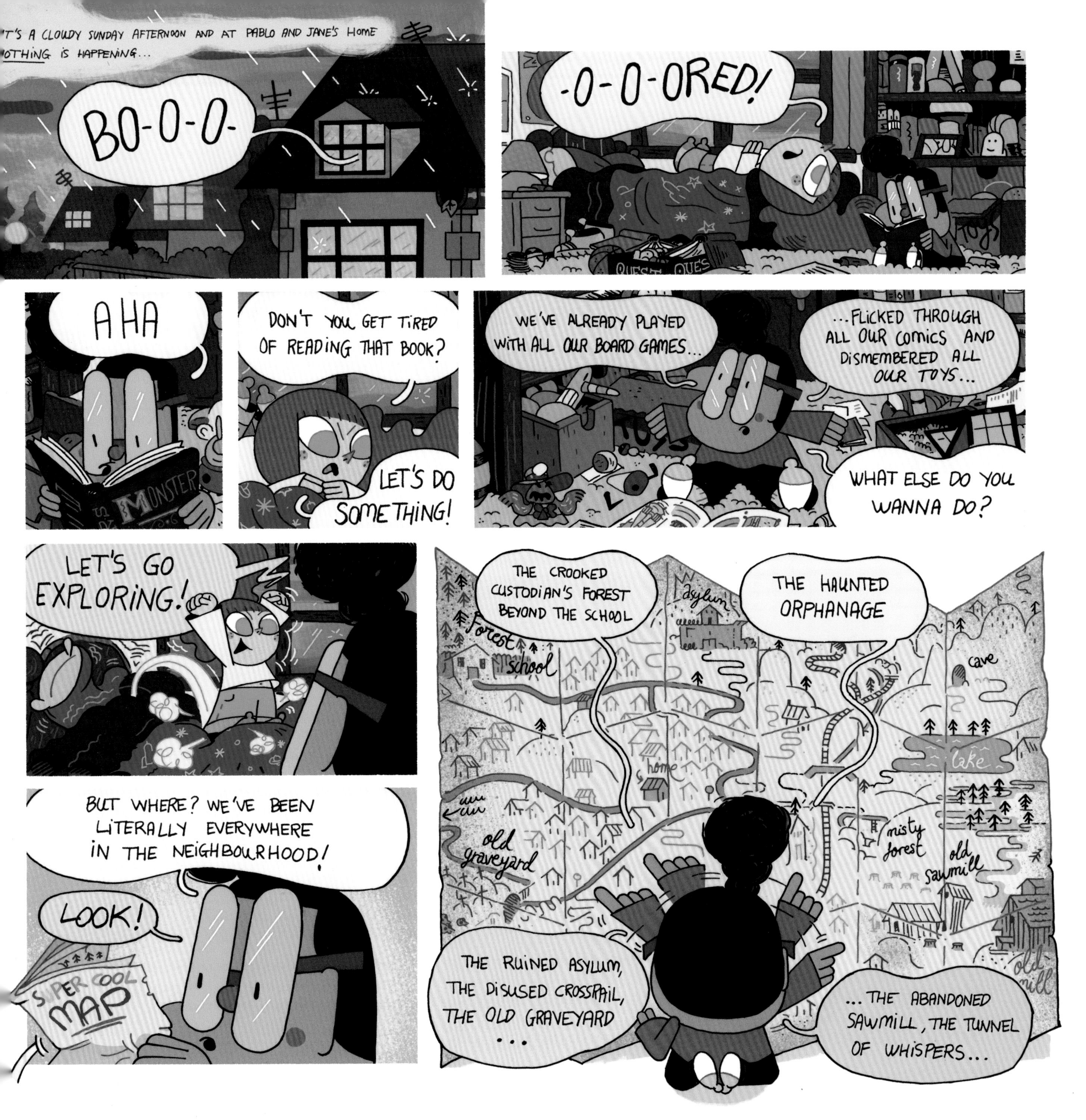
T'S A CLOUDY SUNDAY AFTERNOON AND AT PABLO AND JANE'S HOME OTHING IS HAPPENING...
BO-O-O-
-O-O-ORED!
AHA
MONSTER
DON'T YOU GET TIRED OF READING THAT BOOK?
LET'S DO SOMETHING!
WE'VE ALREADY PLAYED WITH ALL OUR BOARD GAMES...
...FLICKED THROUGH ALL OUR COMICS AND DISMEMBERED ALL OUR TOYS...
WHAT ELSE DO YOU WANNA DO?
LET'S GO EXPLORING!
BUT WHERE? WE'VE BEEN LITERALLY EVERYWHERE IN THE NEIGHBOURHOOD!
LOOK!
SUPER COOL MAP
THE CROOKED CUSTODIAN'S FOREST BEYOND THE SCHOOL
THE HAUNTED ORPHANAGE
forest
school
asylum
cave
home
lake
old graveyard
misty forest
old sawmill
old mill
THE RUINED ASYLUM, THE DISUSED CROSSRAIL, THE OLD GRAVEYARD ...
... THE ABANDONED SAWMILL, THE TUNNEL OF WHISPERS...

NOT EVERYTHING!

OVER THERE!

THE OLD HOUSE ON THE HILL?

YUP!

B-B-BUT... ALL THE KIDS AT SCHOOL SAY THAT IT'S FILLED WITH MONSTERS...

YEPPERS!

AND YOU SEE THAT GREEN GLOW THAT'S COMING FROM THE BACK GARDEN?

T-T-THAT'S BECAUSE OF THE RADIOACTIVE METEORITE THAT CRASHED THERE YEARS AGO...

YES!

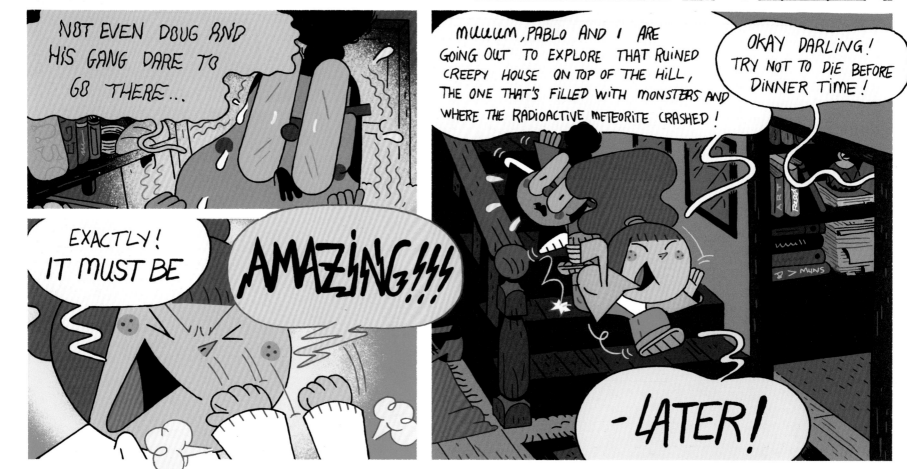
NOT EVEN DOUG AND HIS GANG DARE TO GO THERE...

EXACTLY! IT MUST BE AMAZING!!!

MUUUM, PABLO AND I ARE GOING OUT TO EXPLORE THAT RUINED CREEPY HOUSE ON TOP OF THE HILL, THE ONE THAT'S FILLED WITH MONSTERS AND WHERE THE RADIOACTIVE METEORITE CRASHED!

OKAY DARLING! TRY NOT TO DIE BEFORE DINNER TIME!

-LATER!

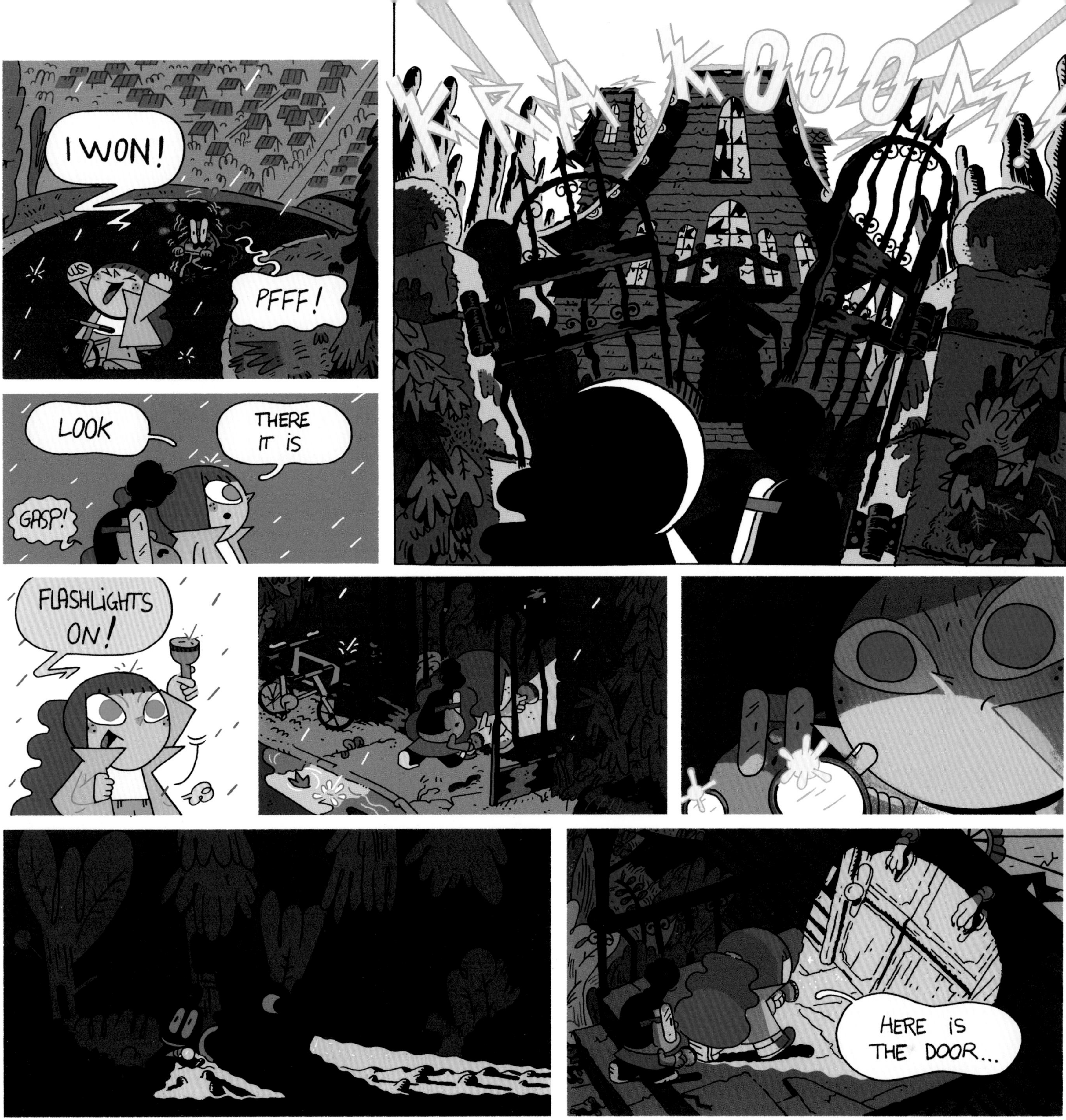
I WON!
PFFF!
LOOK
THERE IT IS
GASP!
KRAKOOOM!!
FLASHLIGHTS ON!
HERE IS THE DOOR...

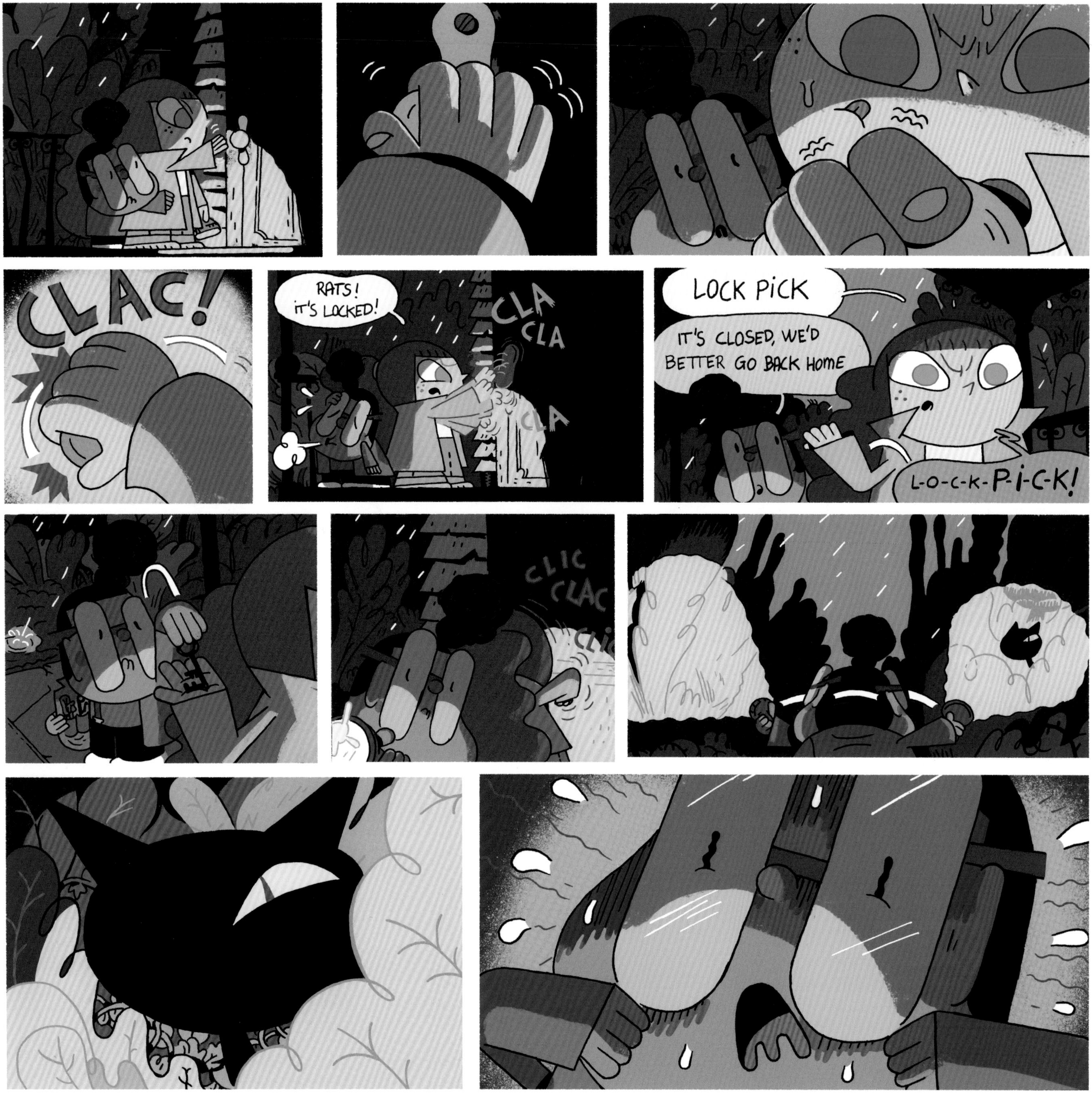
CLAC!
RATS! IT'S LOCKED!
CLA
CLA
CLA
LOCK PICK
IT'S CLOSED, WE'D BETTER GO BACK HOME
L-O-C-K-P-I-C-K!
CLIC
CLAC
CLIC

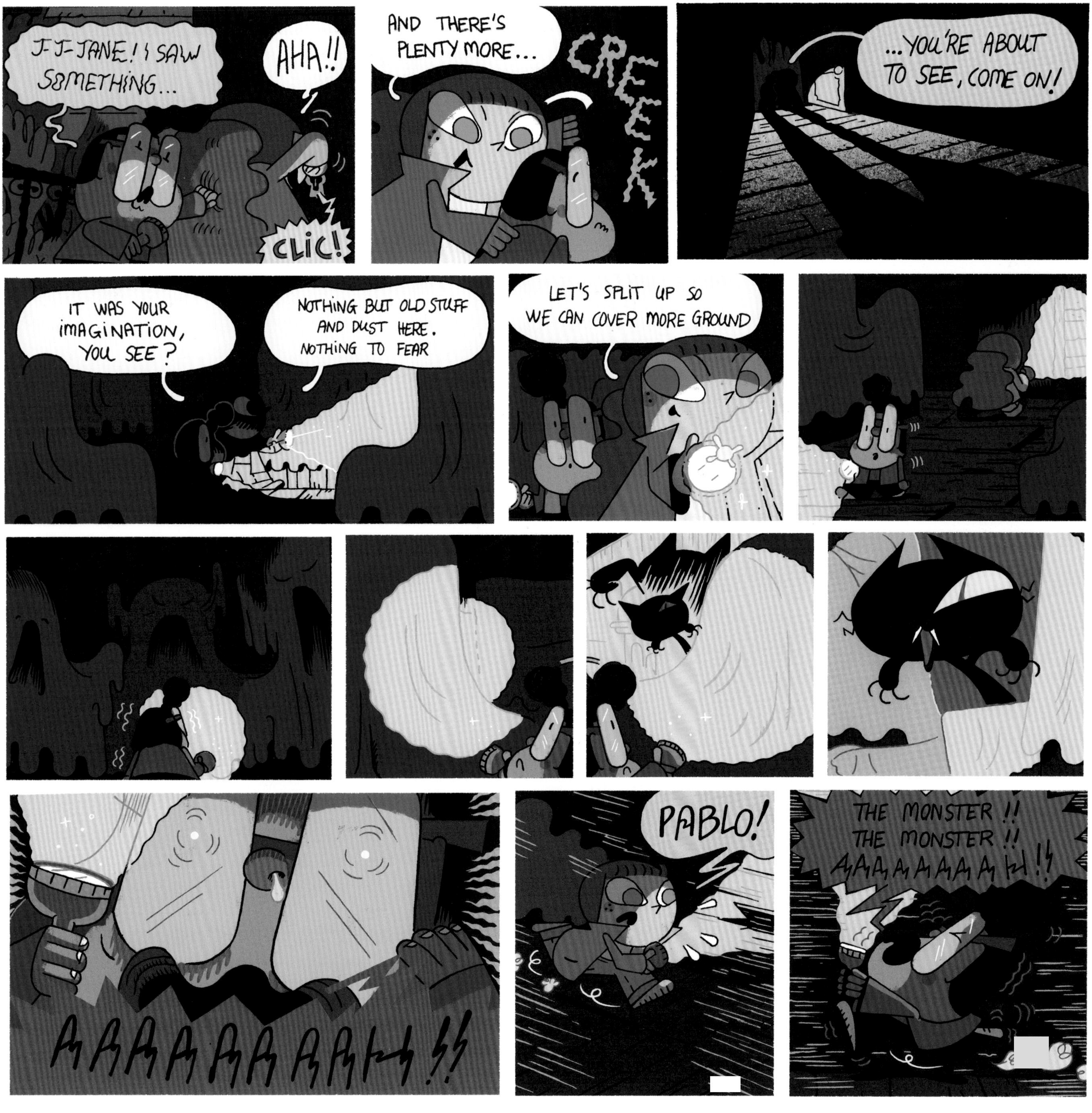
J-J-JANE! I SAW SOMETHING...
AHA!!
CLIC!
AND THERE'S PLENTY MORE...
CREEEK
...YOU'RE ABOUT TO SEE, COME ON!
IT WAS YOUR IMAGINATION, YOU SEE?
NOTHING BUT OLD STUFF AND DUST HERE. NOTHING TO FEAR
LET'S SPLIT UP SO WE CAN COVER MORE GROUND
AAAAAAAAAHH!!
PABLO!
THE MONSTER!!
THE MONSTER!!
AAAAAAAAAH!!

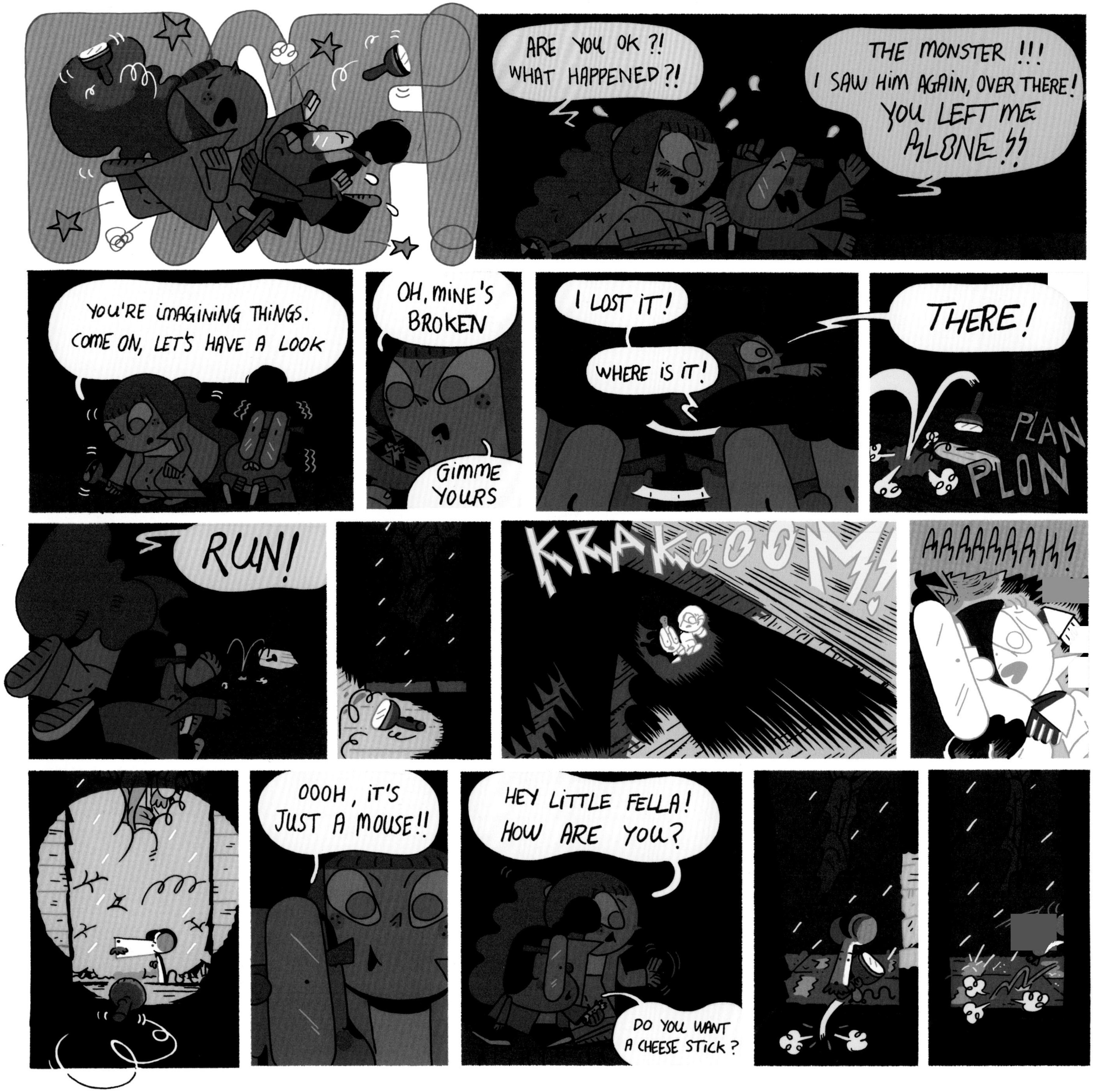

ARE YOU OK ?! WHAT HAPPENED ?!
THE MONSTER !!! I SAW HIM AGAIN, OVER THERE! YOU LEFT ME ALONE !!
YOU'RE IMAGINING THINGS. COME ON, LET'S HAVE A LOOK
OH, MINE'S BROKEN
GIMME YOURS
I LOST IT!
WHERE IS IT!
THERE!
PLAN
PLON
RUN!
KRAKOOOOM!
AAAAAAAH!!
OOOH, IT'S JUST A MOUSE!!
HEY LITTLE FELLA! HOW ARE YOU?
DO YOU WANT A CHEESE STICK?

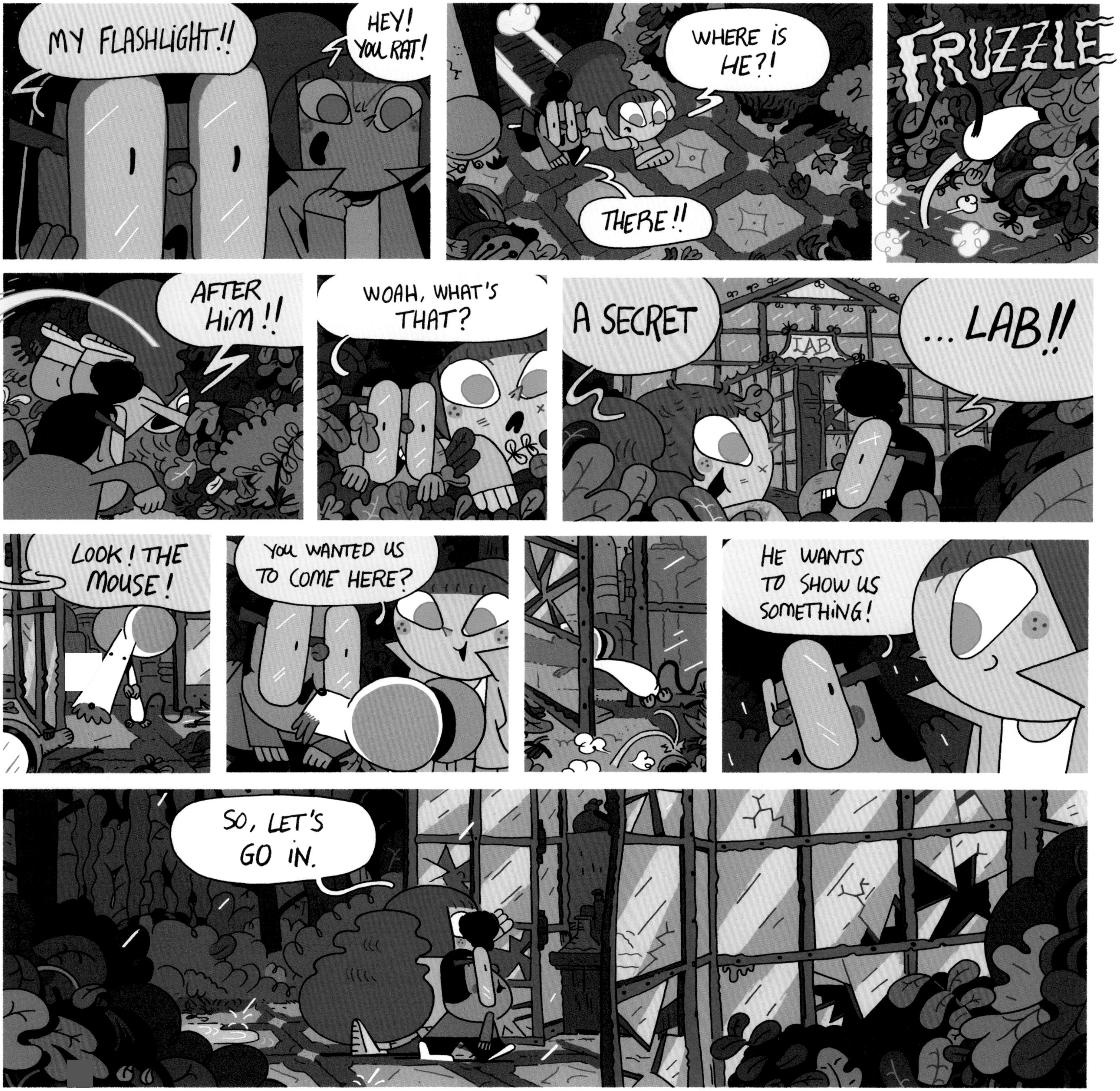
MY FLASHLIGHT!!
HEY! YOU RAT!
WHERE IS HE?!
THERE!!
FRUZZLE
AFTER HIM!!
WOAH, WHAT'S THAT?
A SECRET
...LAB!!
LAB
LOOK! THE MOUSE!
YOU WANTED US TO COME HERE?
HE WANTS TO SHOW US SOMETHING!
SO, LET'S GO IN.

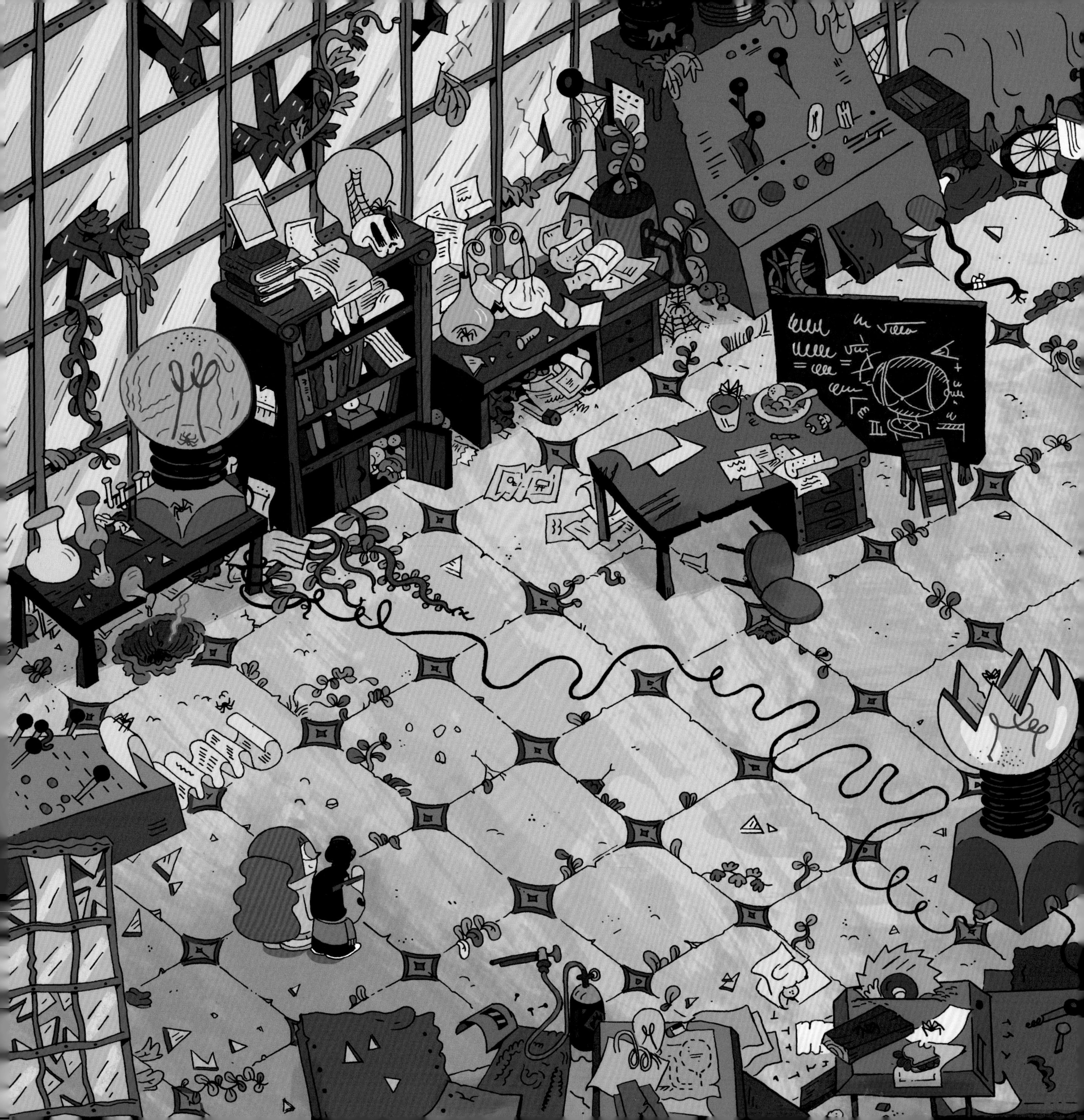

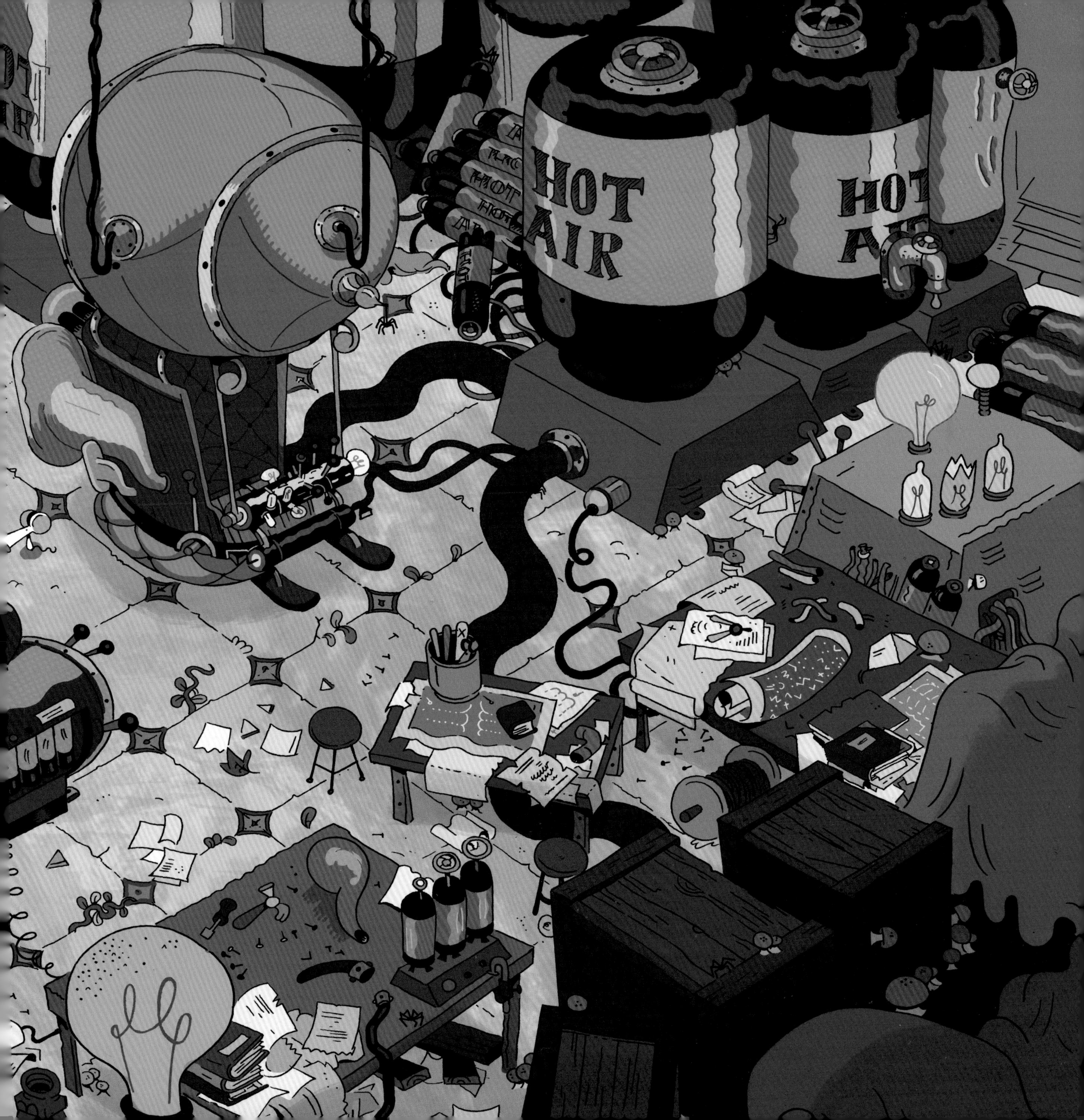
HOT
AIR

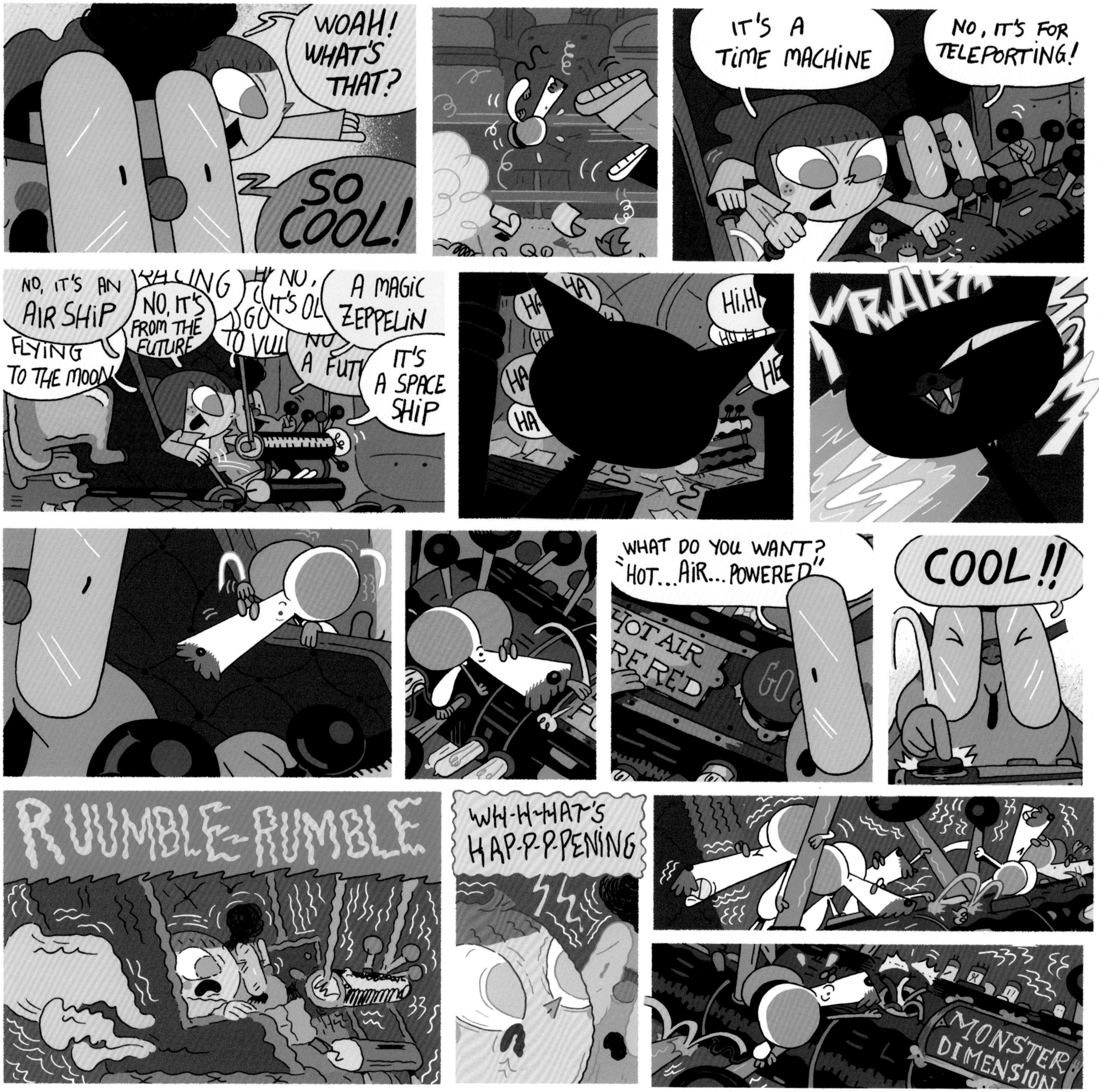
WOAH! WHAT'S THAT?
SO COOL!
IT'S A TIME MACHINE
NO, IT'S FOR TELEPORTING!
NO, IT'S AN AIR SHIP FLYING TO THE MOON
NO, IT'S FROM THE FUTURE
A MAGIC ZEPPELIN
IT'S A SPACE SHIP
WHAT DO YOU WANT? "HOT...AIR...POWERED"
HOT AIR
COOL!!
RUUMBLE RUMBLE
WH-H-HAT'S HAP-P-P-PENING
MONSTER DIMENSION

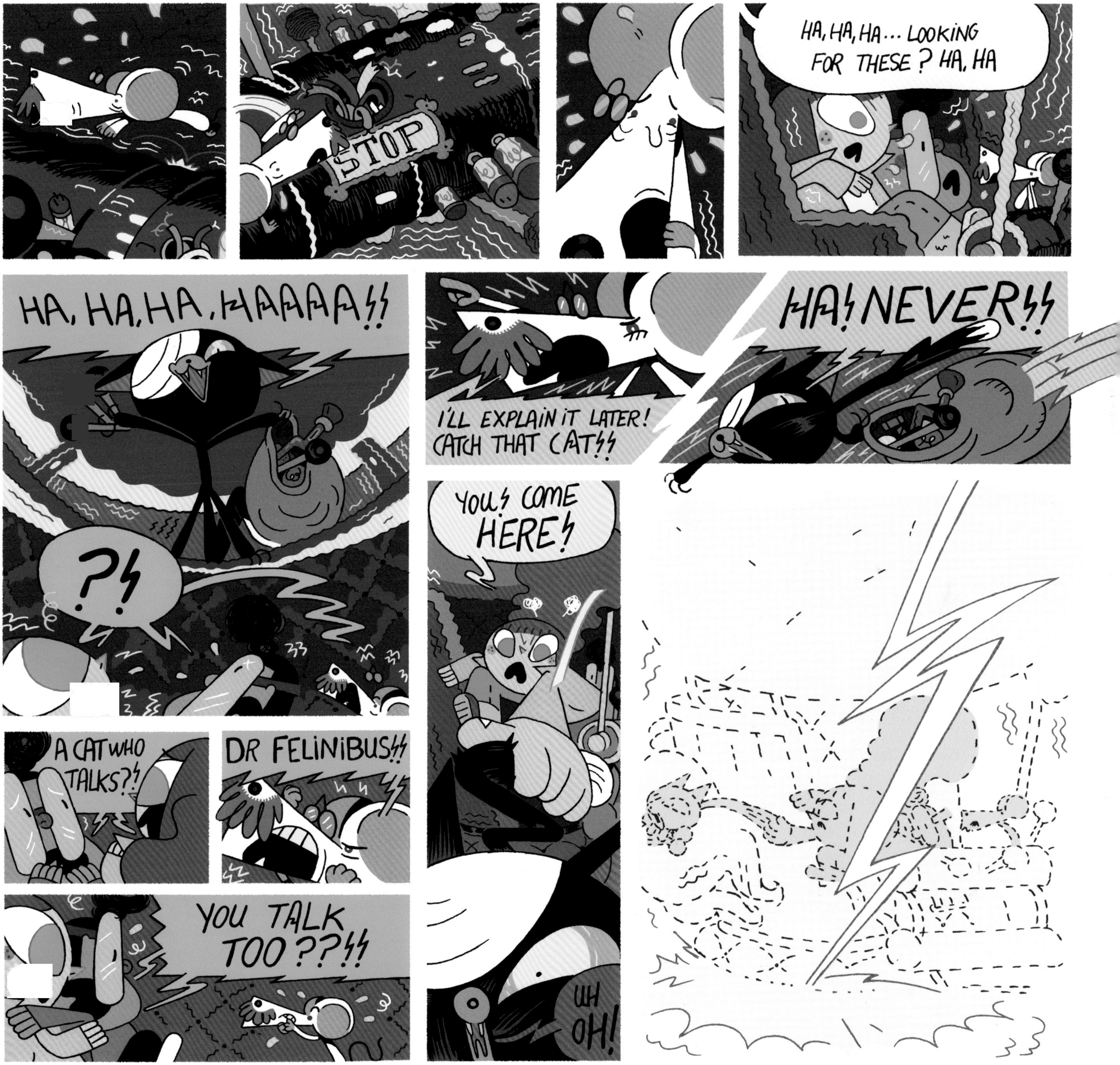
STOP
HA, HA, HA... LOOKING FOR THESE? HA, HA
HA, HA, HA, HAAAAA!!
?!
I'LL EXPLAIN IT LATER! CATCH THAT CAT!!
HA! NEVER!!
A CAT WHO TALKS?!
DR FELINIBUS!!
YOU TALK TOO??!!
YOU! COME HERE!
UH OH!

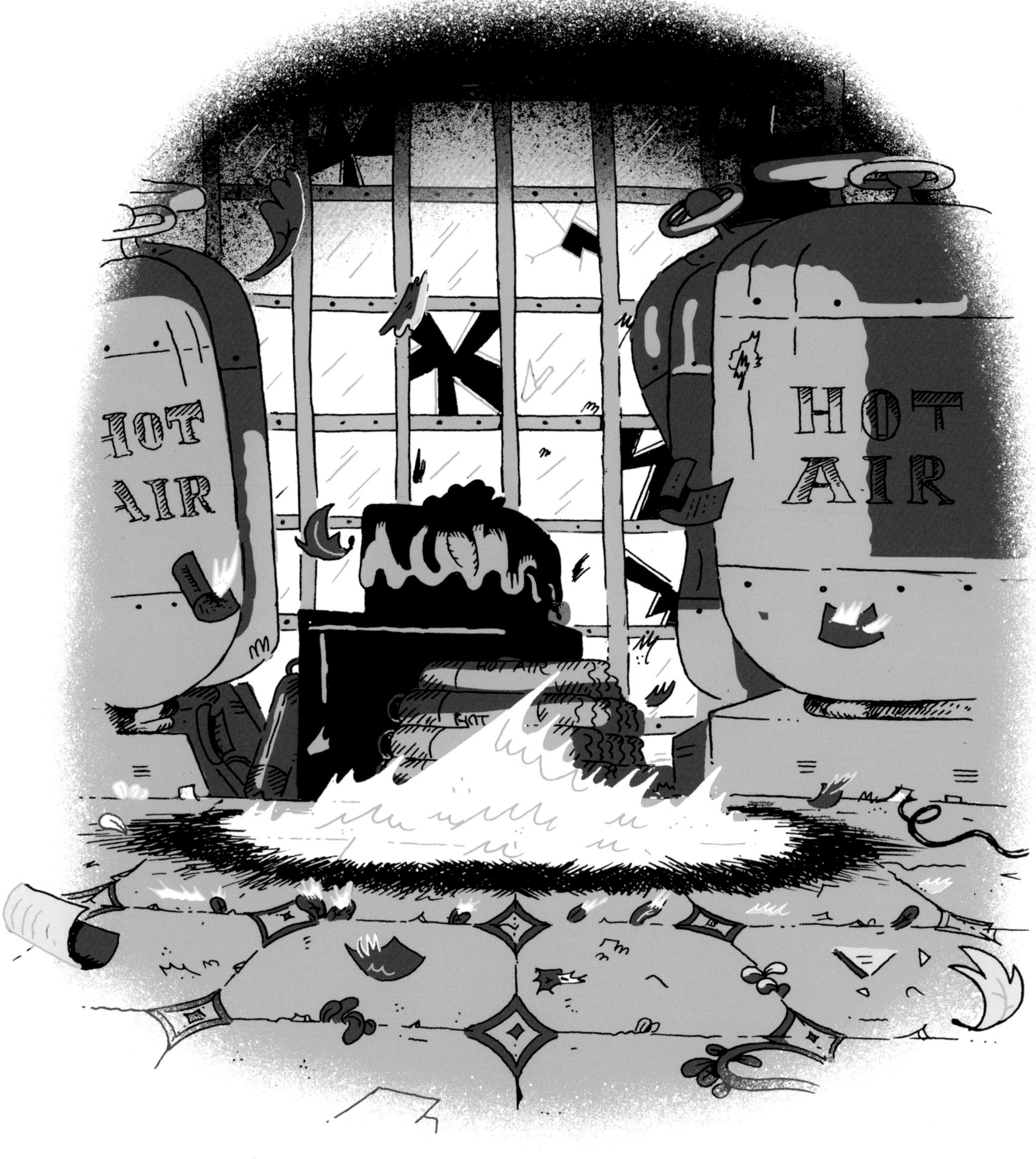
HOT AIR
HOT AIR

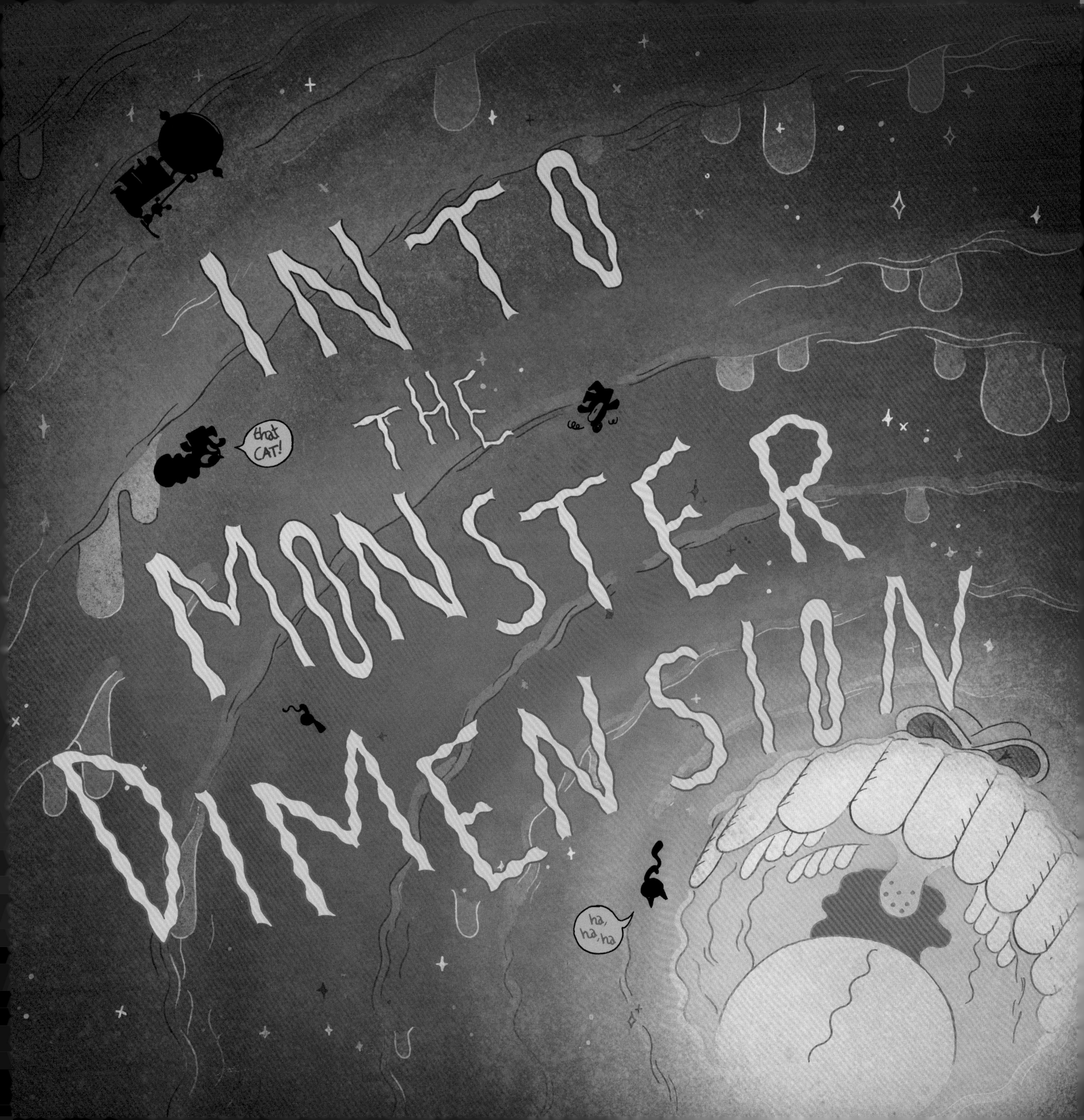

INTO THE MONSTER DIMENSION
that CAT!
ha, ha, ha

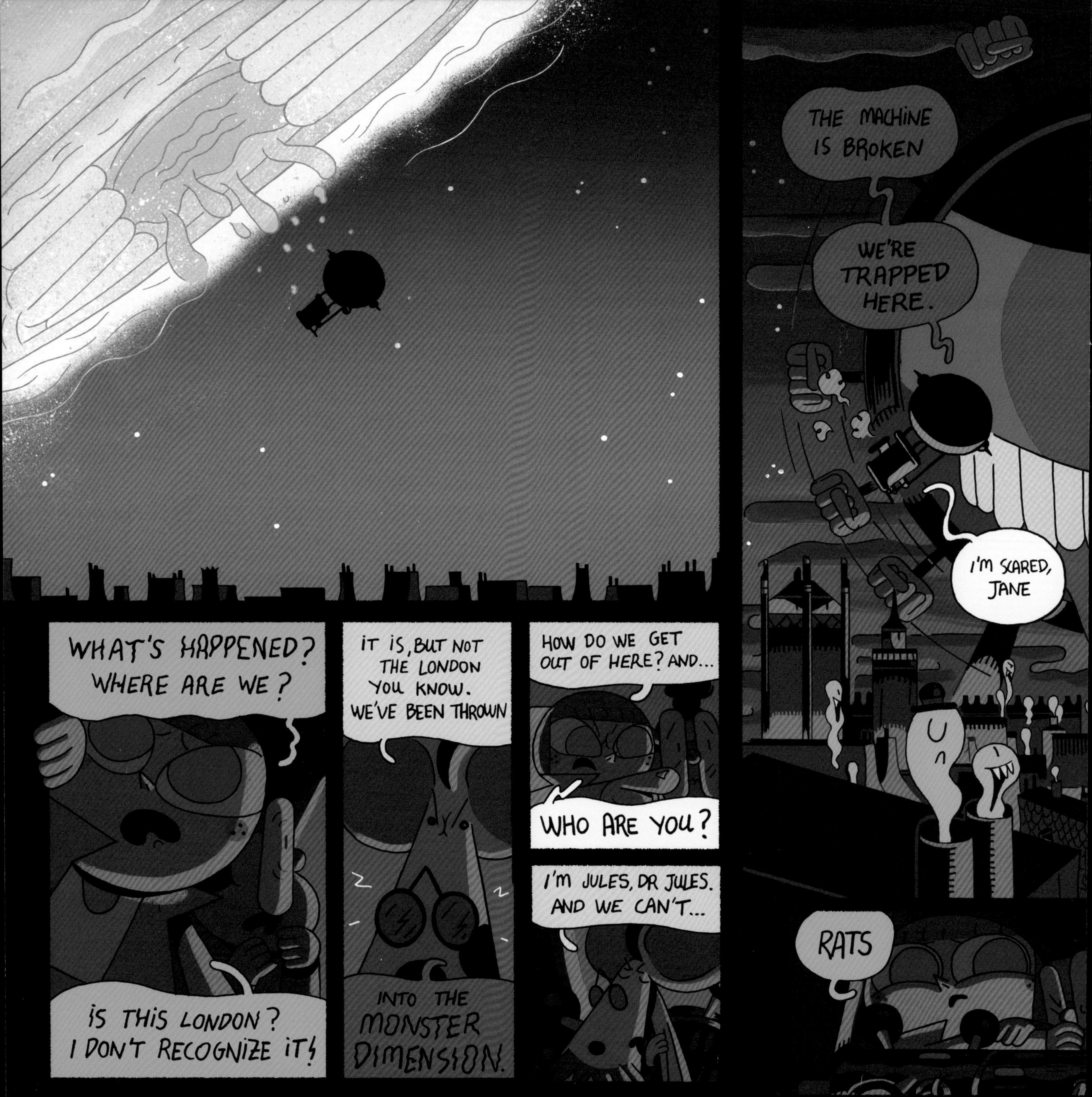
WHAT'S HAPPENED? WHERE ARE WE?
IS THIS LONDON? I DON'T RECOGNIZE IT!
IT IS, BUT NOT THE LONDON YOU KNOW. WE'VE BEEN THROWN
INTO THE MONSTER DIMENSION.
HOW DO WE GET OUT OF HERE? AND...
WHO ARE YOU?
I'M JULES, DR JULES. AND WE CAN'T...
THE MACHINE IS BROKEN
WE'RE TRAPPED HERE.
I'M SCARED, JANE
RATS

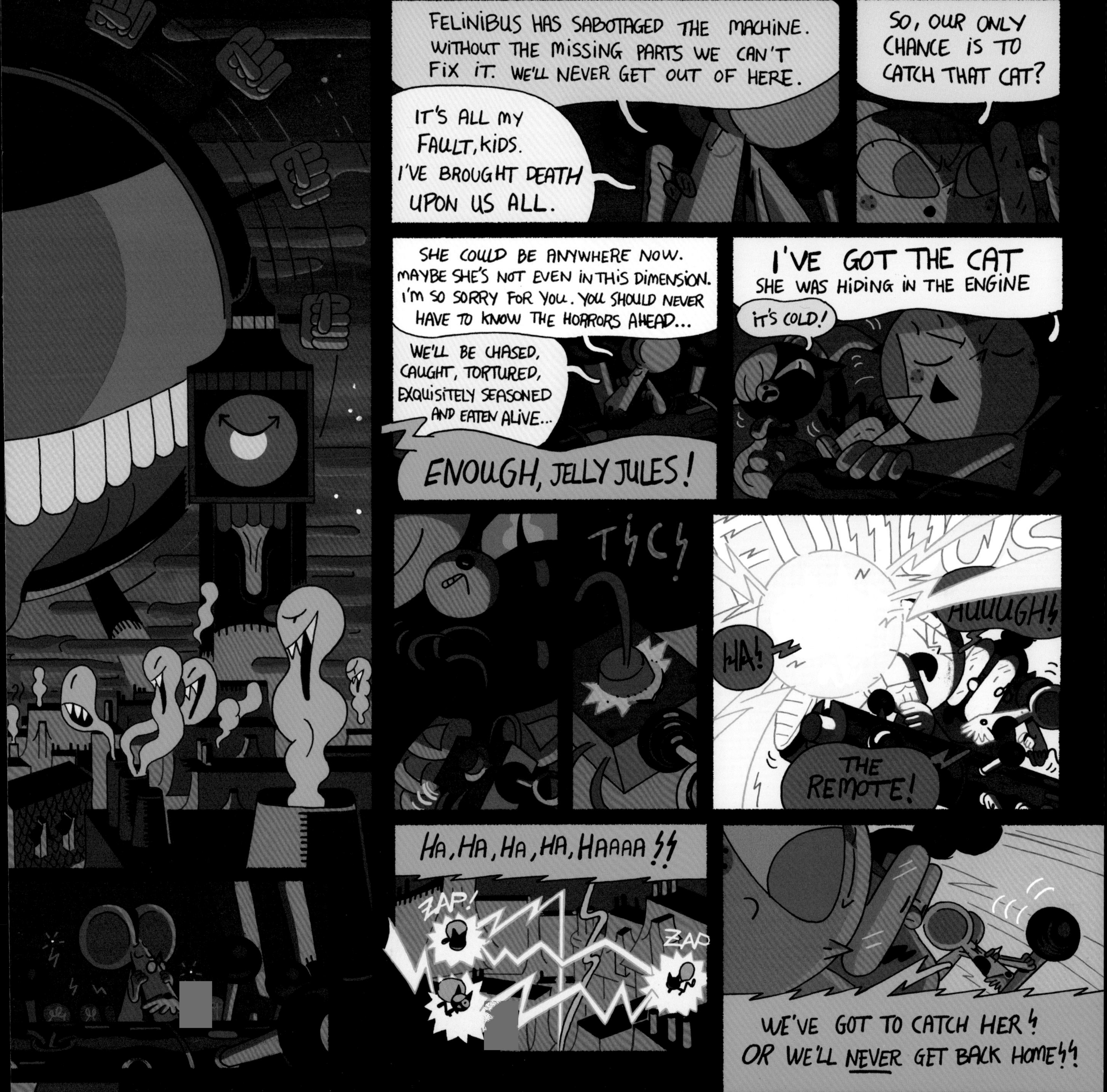
FELINIBUS HAS SABOTAGED THE MACHINE. WITHOUT THE MISSING PARTS WE CAN'T FIX IT. WE'LL NEVER GET OUT OF HERE.
IT'S ALL MY FAULT, KIDS. I'VE BROUGHT DEATH UPON US ALL.
SO, OUR ONLY CHANCE IS TO CATCH THAT CAT?
SHE COULD BE ANYWHERE NOW. MAYBE SHE'S NOT EVEN IN THIS DIMENSION. I'M SO SORRY FOR YOU. YOU SHOULD NEVER HAVE TO KNOW THE HORRORS AHEAD...
WE'LL BE CHASED, CAUGHT, TORTURED, EXQUISITELY SEASONED AND EATEN ALIVE...
ENOUGH, JELLY JULES!
I'VE GOT THE CAT
SHE WAS HIDING IN THE ENGINE
IT'S COLD!
TICS!
HA!
AUUUGH!
THE REMOTE!
HA, HA, HA, HA, HAAAA!!
ZAP!
ZAP
WE'VE GOT TO CATCH HER! OR WE'LL NEVER GET BACK HOME!!

LOPSIDED LONDON

Dr Felinibus has sabotaged our machine! We can't get out of the Monster Dimension without finding the missing parts and fixing the Hot Air Time Contraption! Help us find the missing machine part in Lopsided, Lethal London and catch up with that felonious feline!

You must find:

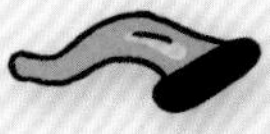

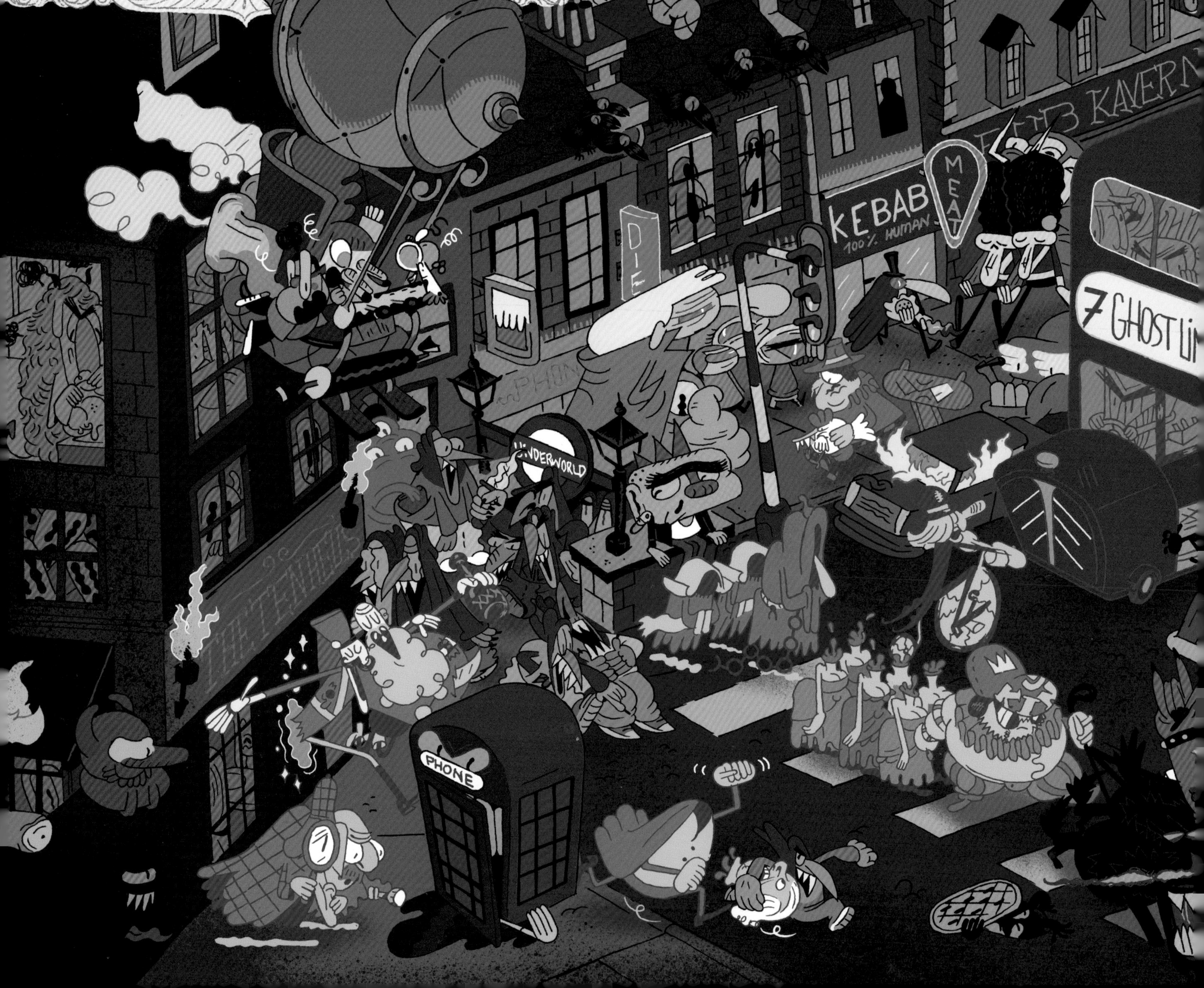
KEBAB
100% HUMAN
MEAT
7 GHOST
PHONE

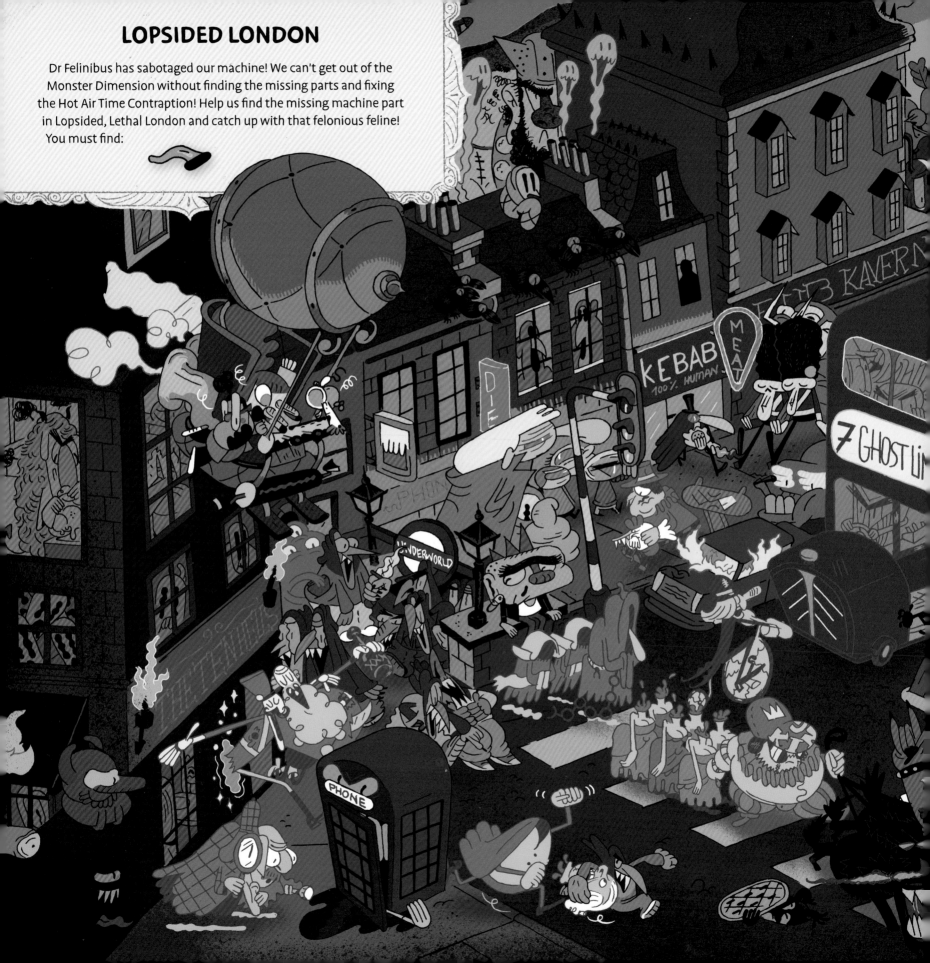

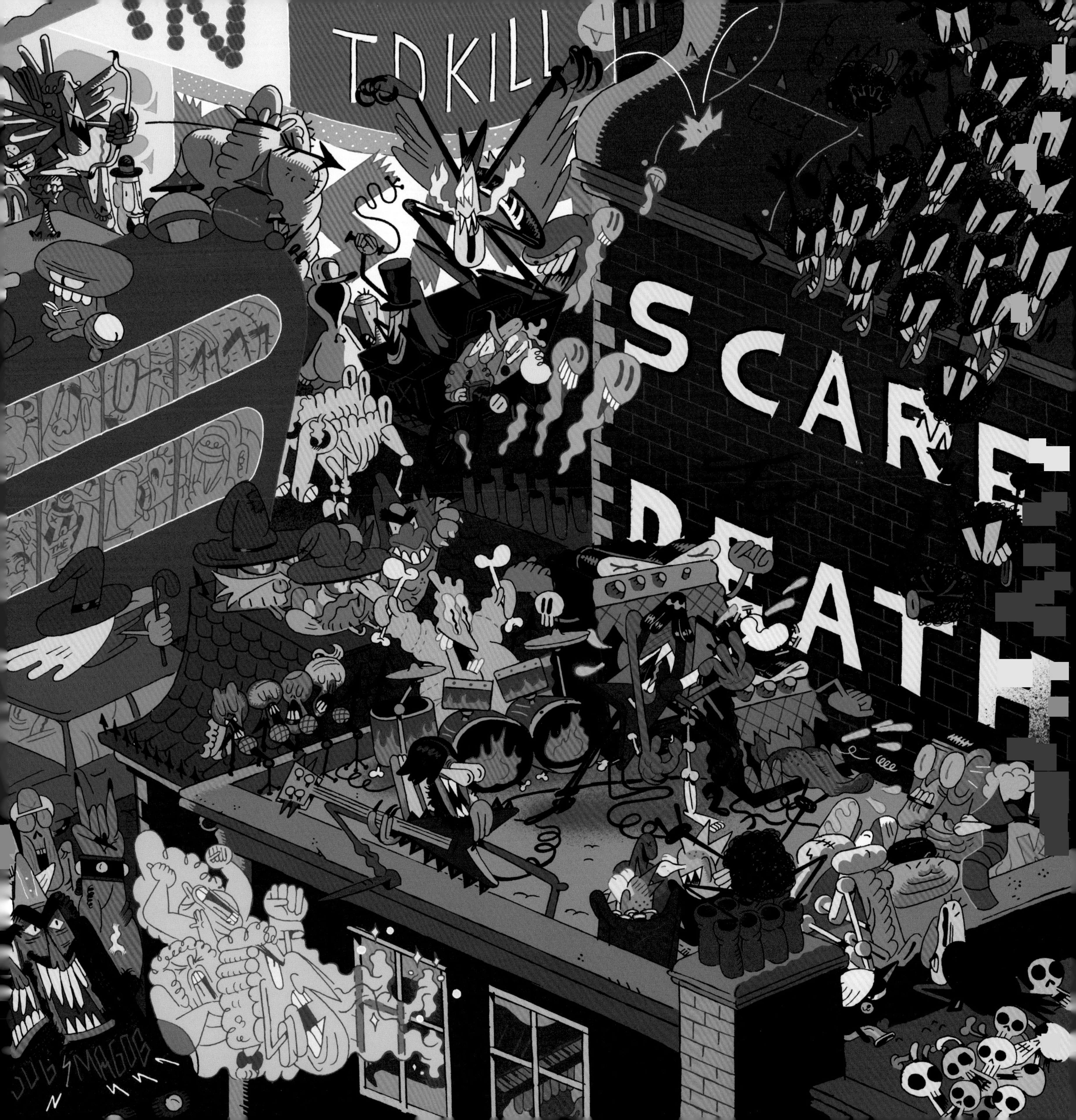
TO KILL
SCARE

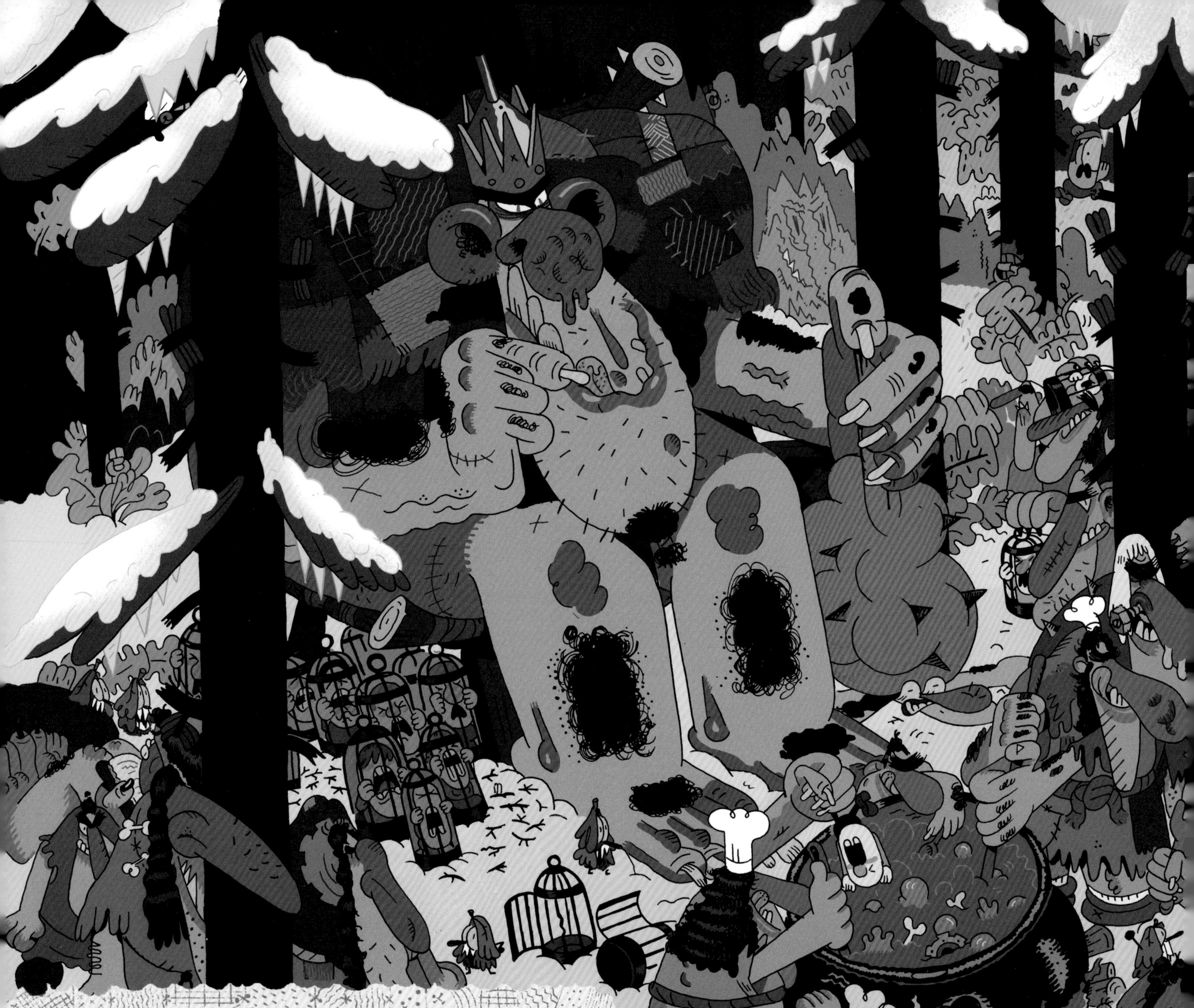

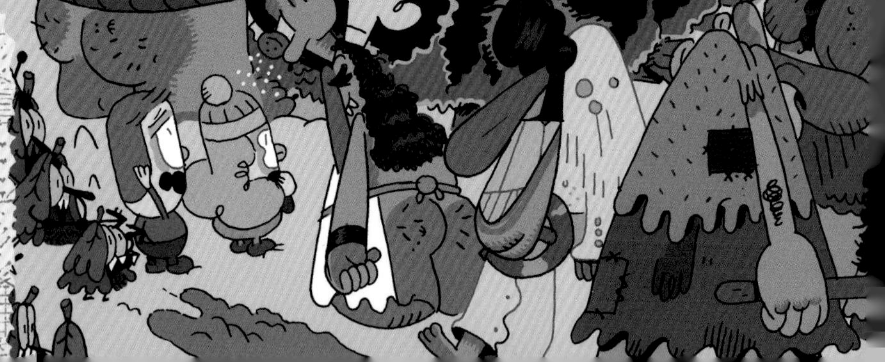

NOCTURNAL NORWAY

Dr Felinibus slipped away in London, but here in Nocturnal Norway, we're sure to see her dark fur against the pale white snow. But beware, at night the trolls turn from stones into child-eating monsters! Dodge the bone-crunching trolls to find:

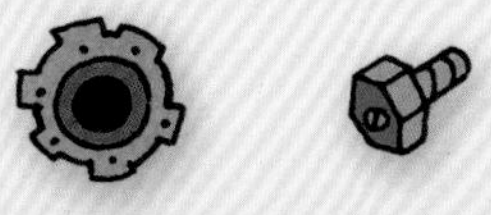

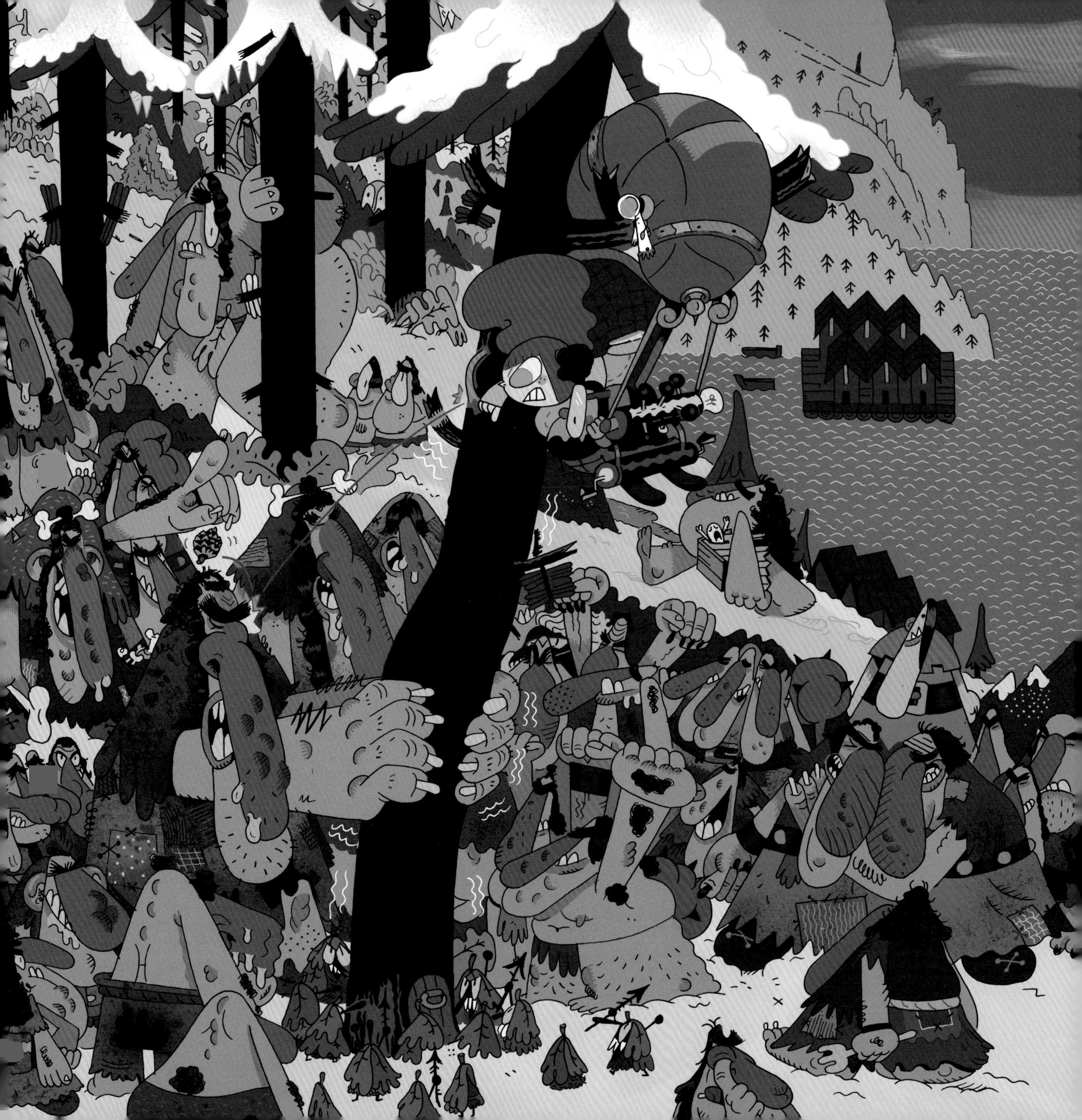

TERRIFYING TRANSYLVANIA

Rats!! She skipped at the last minute! We've tracked Dr Felinibus down to Terrifying Transylvania and we're still far from fixing the Hot Air Time Contraption. Slip by the noxious Nosferatu and the other villainous vampires to find:

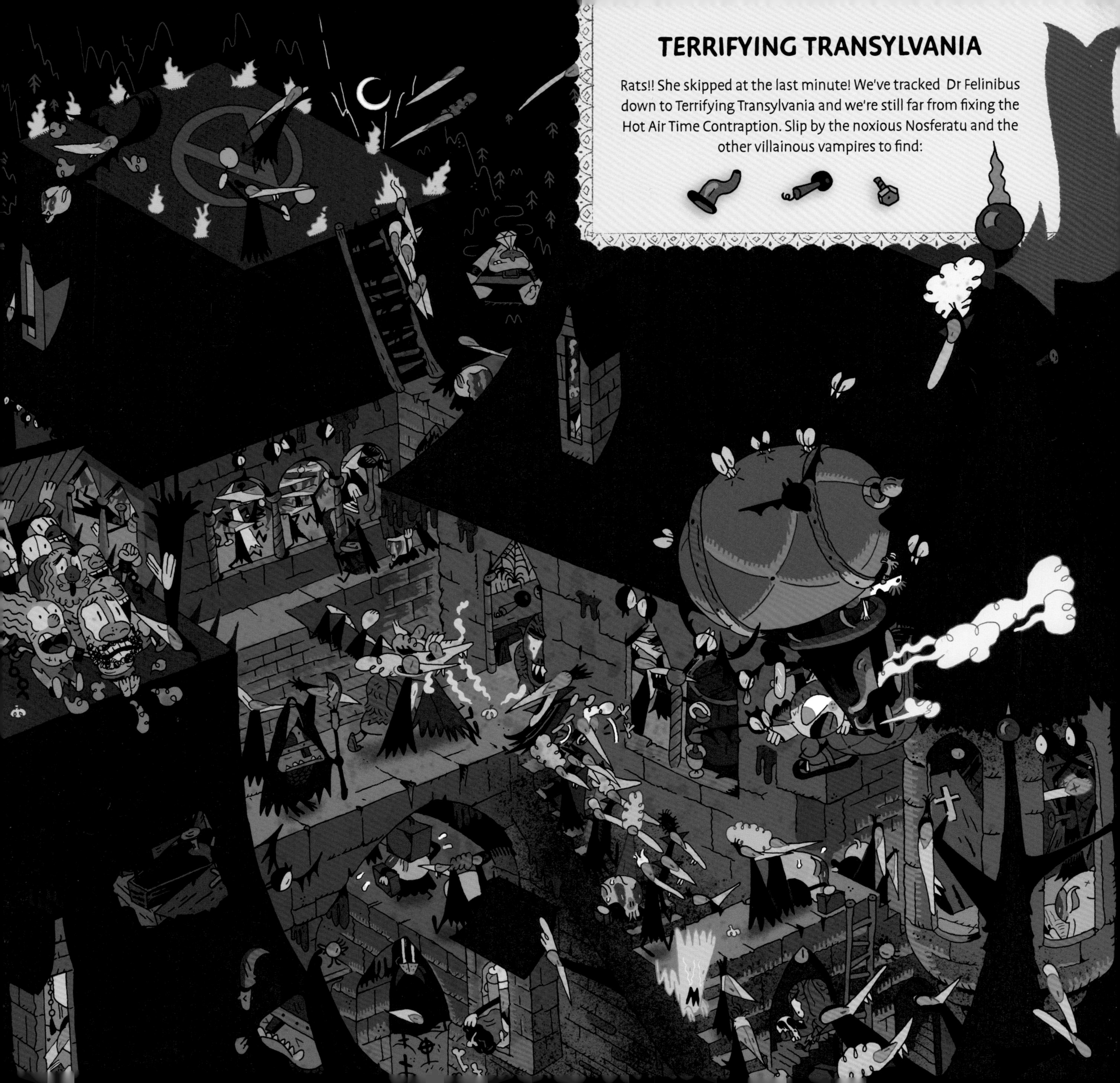

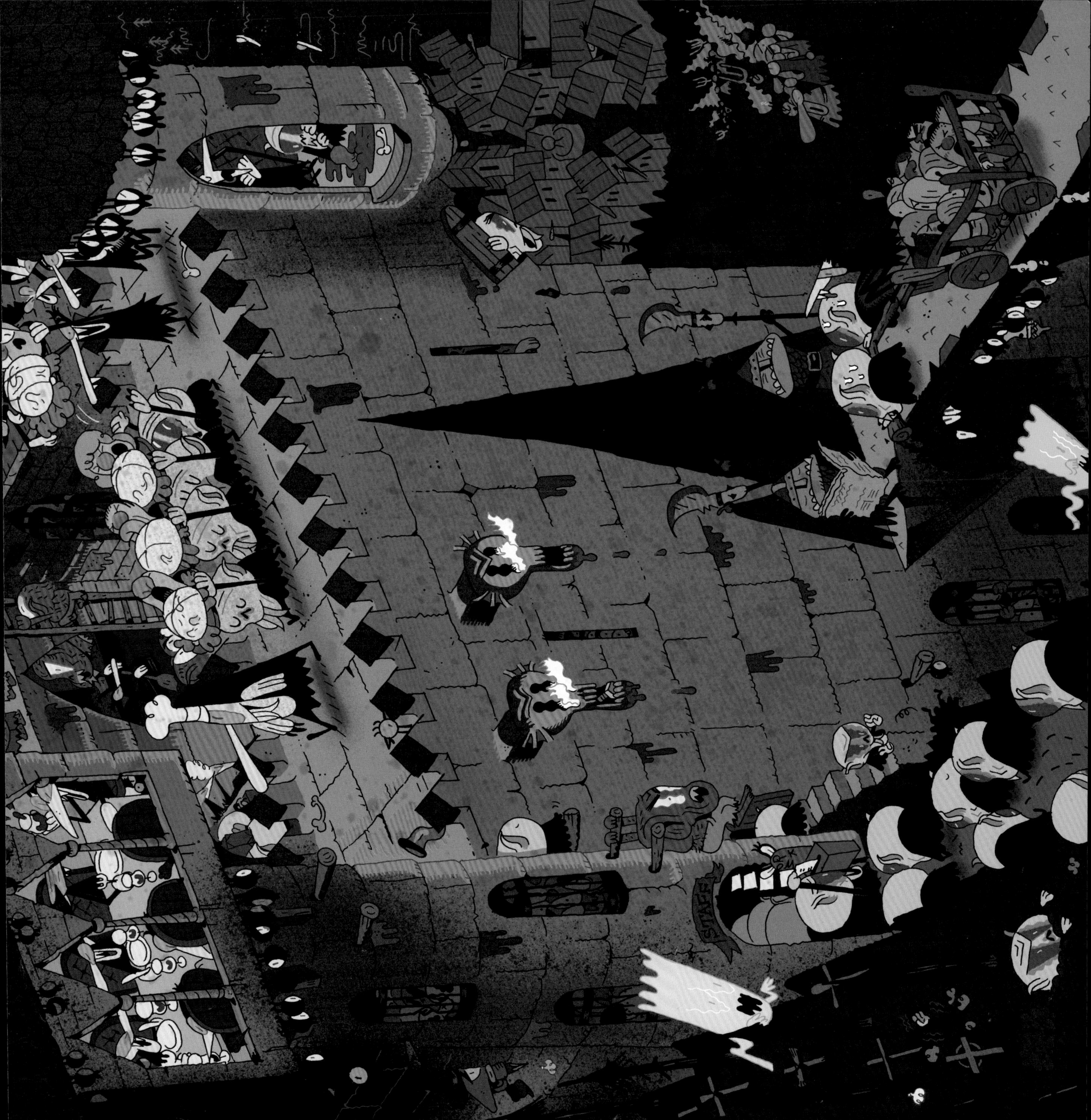
STAFF

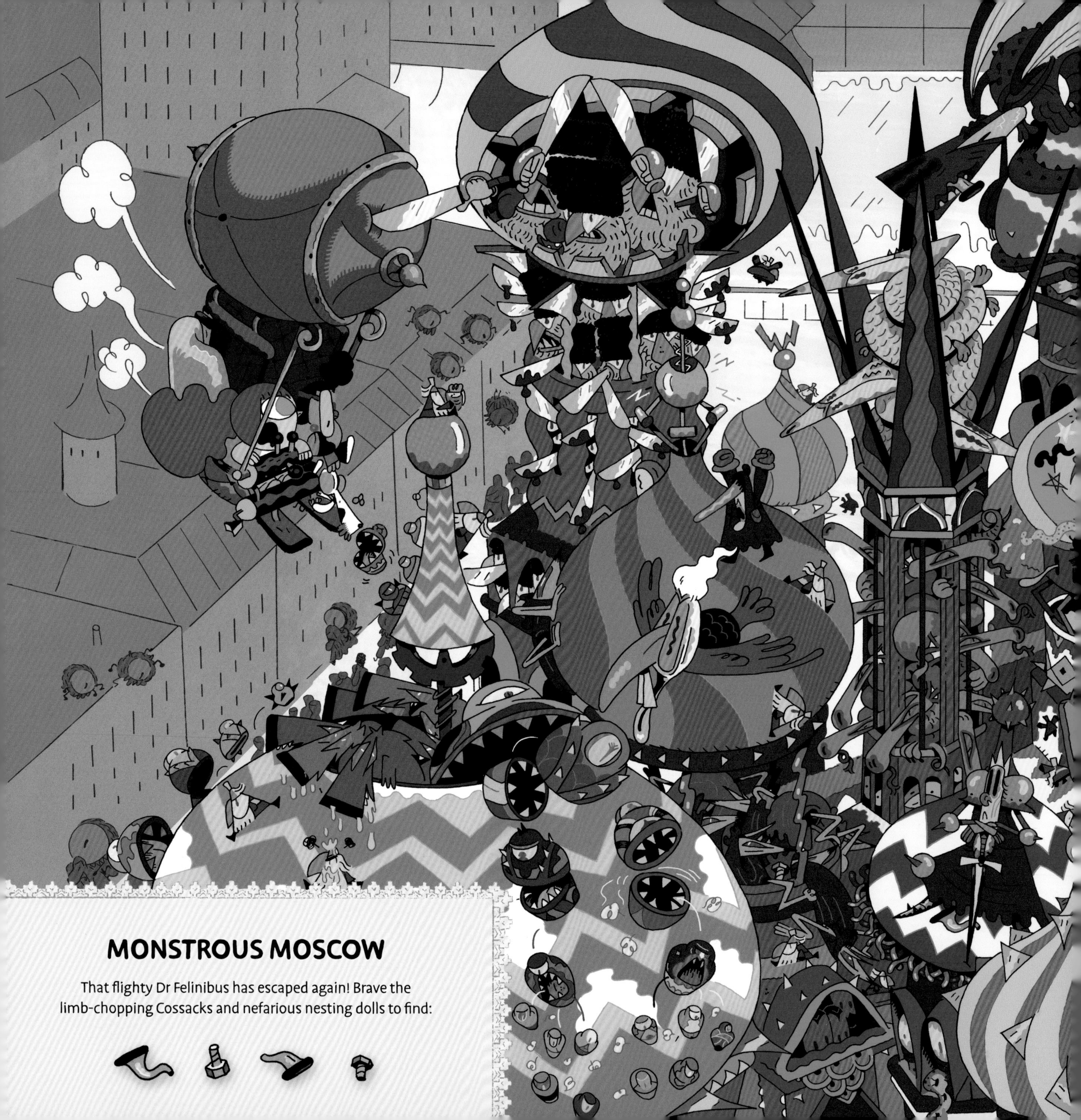

MONSTROUS MOSCOW

That flighty Dr Felinibus has escaped again! Brave the limb-chopping Cossacks and nefarious nesting dolls to find:

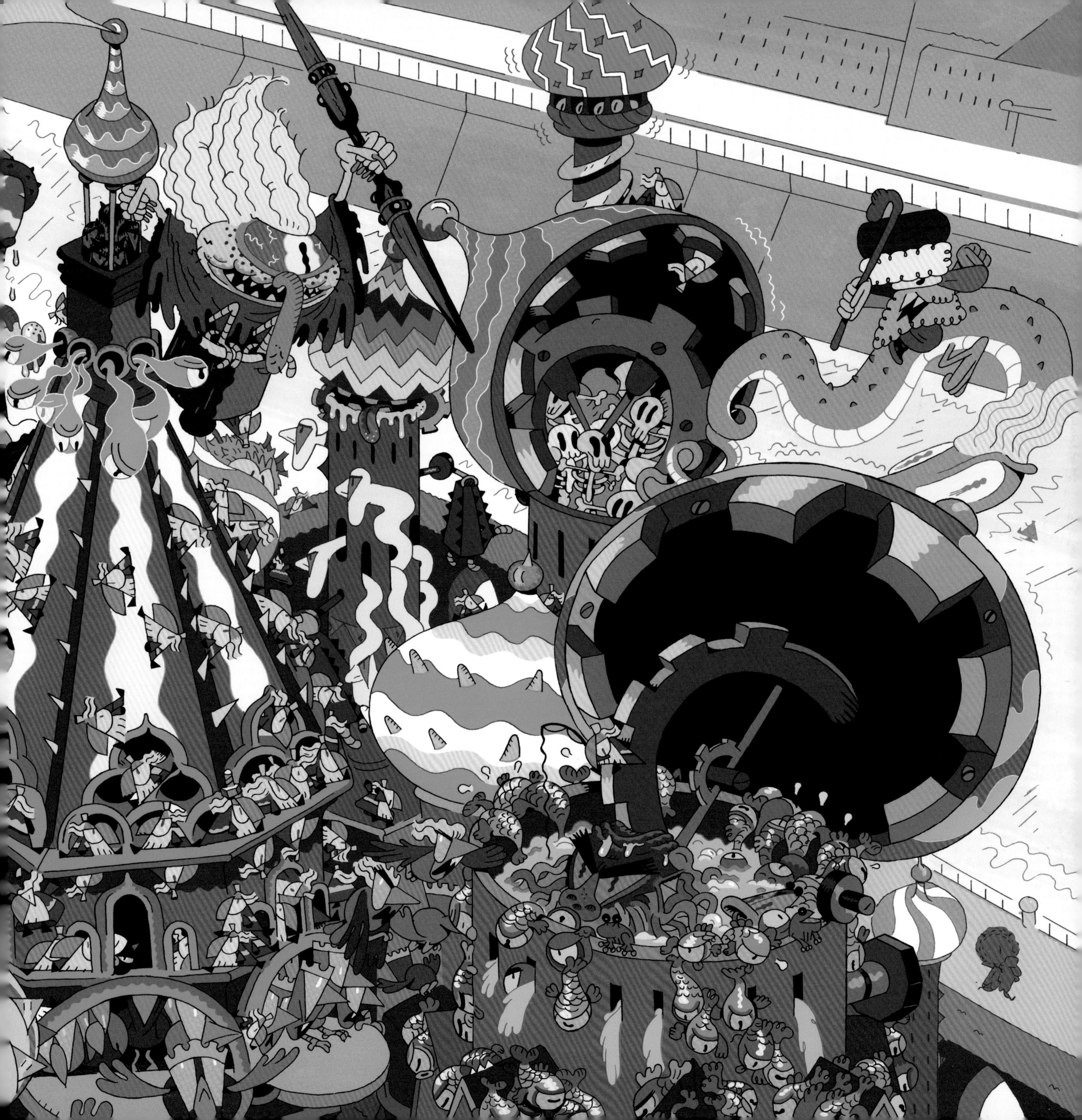

AGELESS ATHENS

Where is she now?! Behold the marvels of Ageless Athens, where immortal gods and mythical monsters recite poetry and democratically debate about the best way to EAT YOU!! You must find:

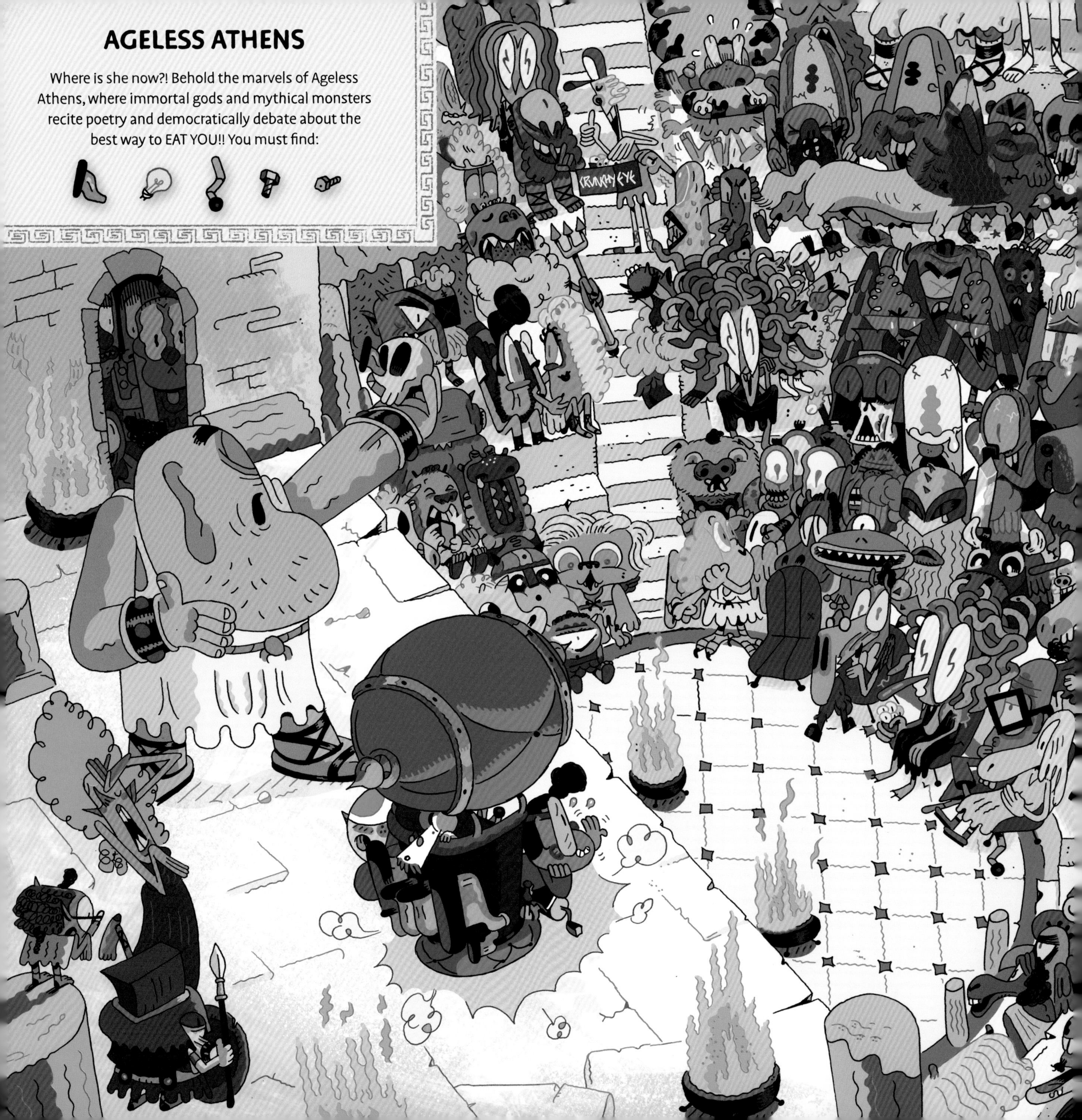
CRUNCHY EYE

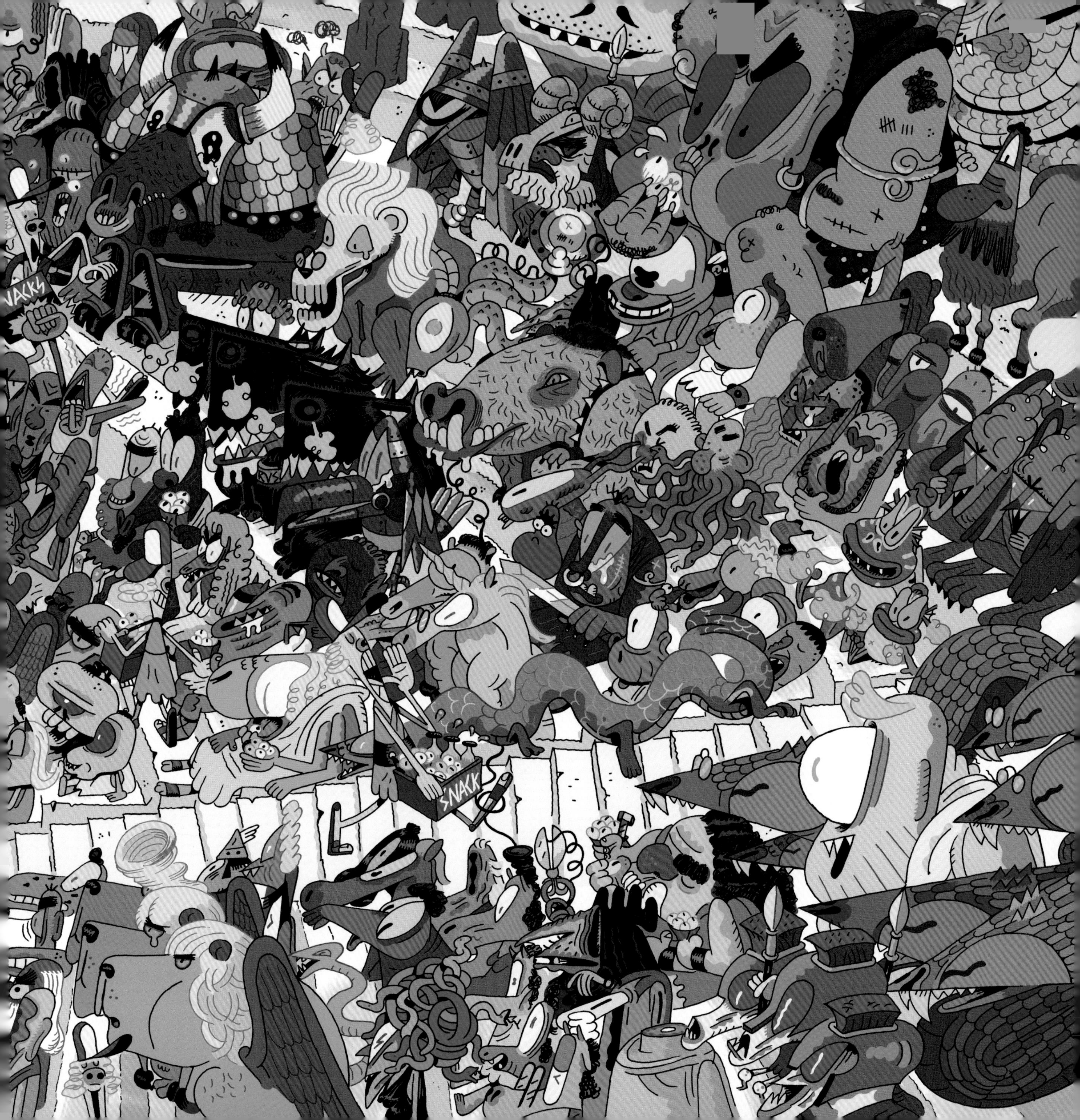
NACKS
SNACK

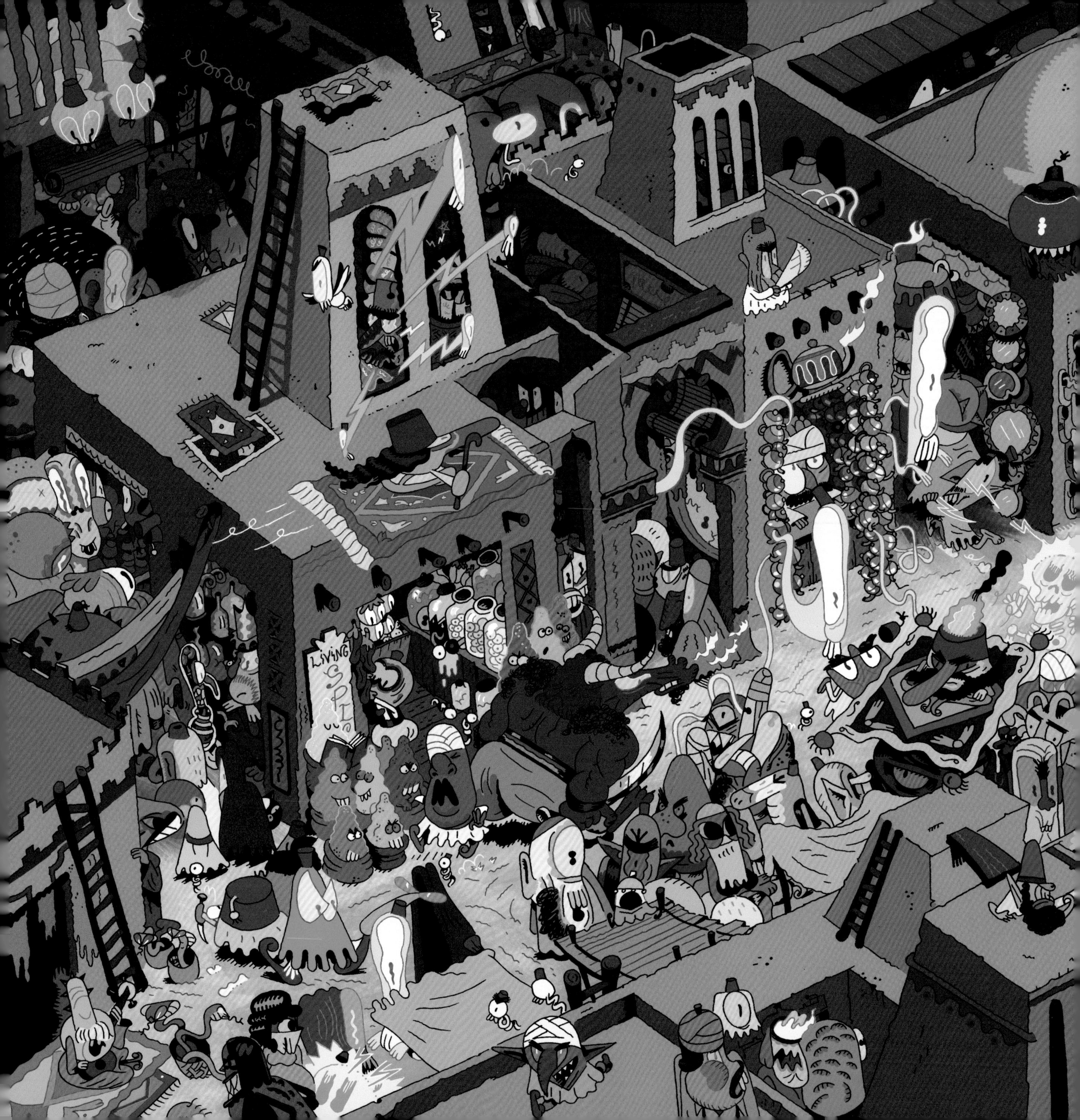
LIVING

MACABRE MARRAKECH

SSSSSSSnakes and ladders everywhere! In Macabre Marrakech the Grand Bazaar is a great place to get lost if you're a bony black cat. It's also a good place to go shopping... for a chopping! Duck the knives of the crooked Khalif's guards and creep around the cobra's fatal fangs to find:

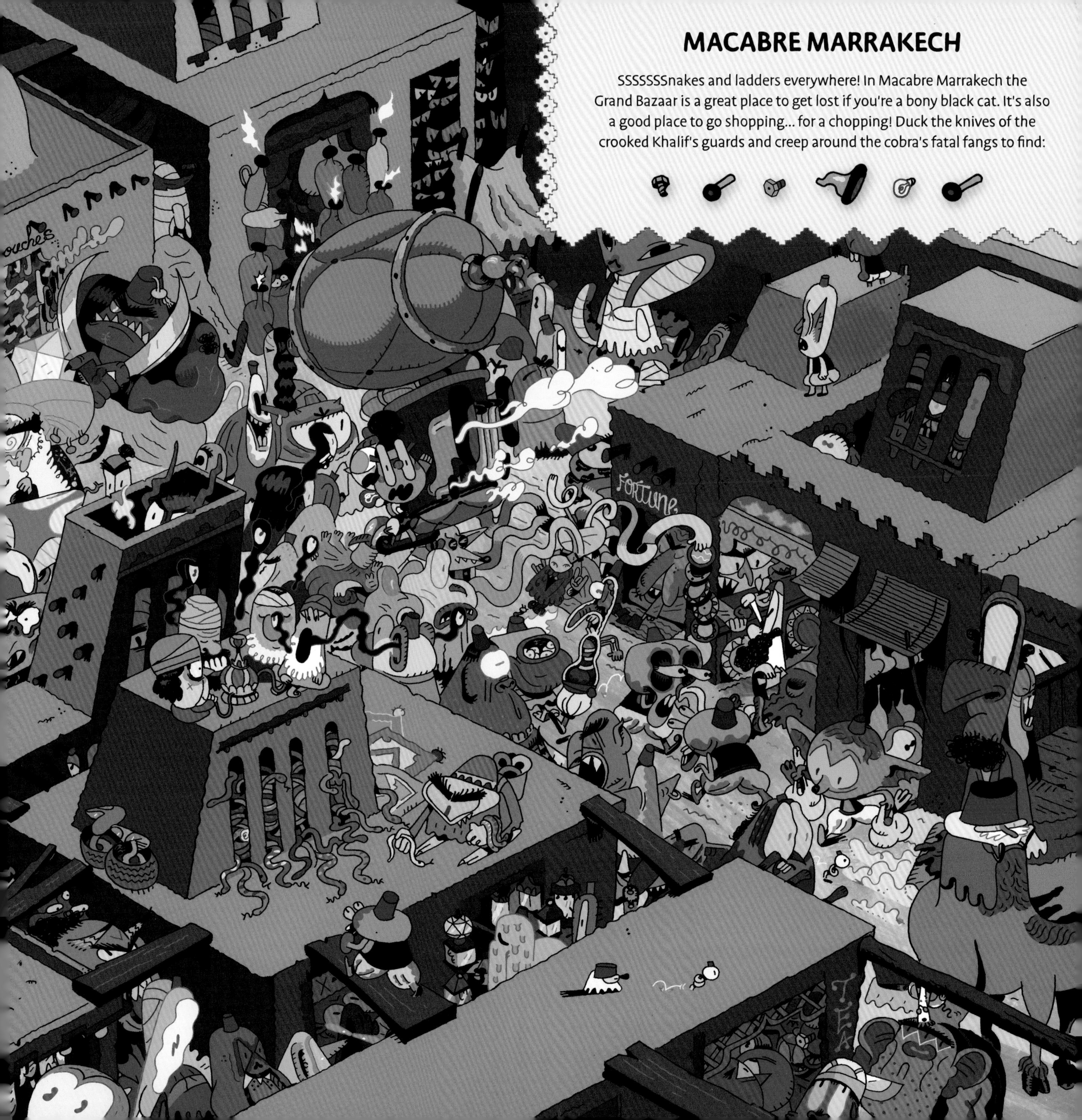
FORTUNE
TEA

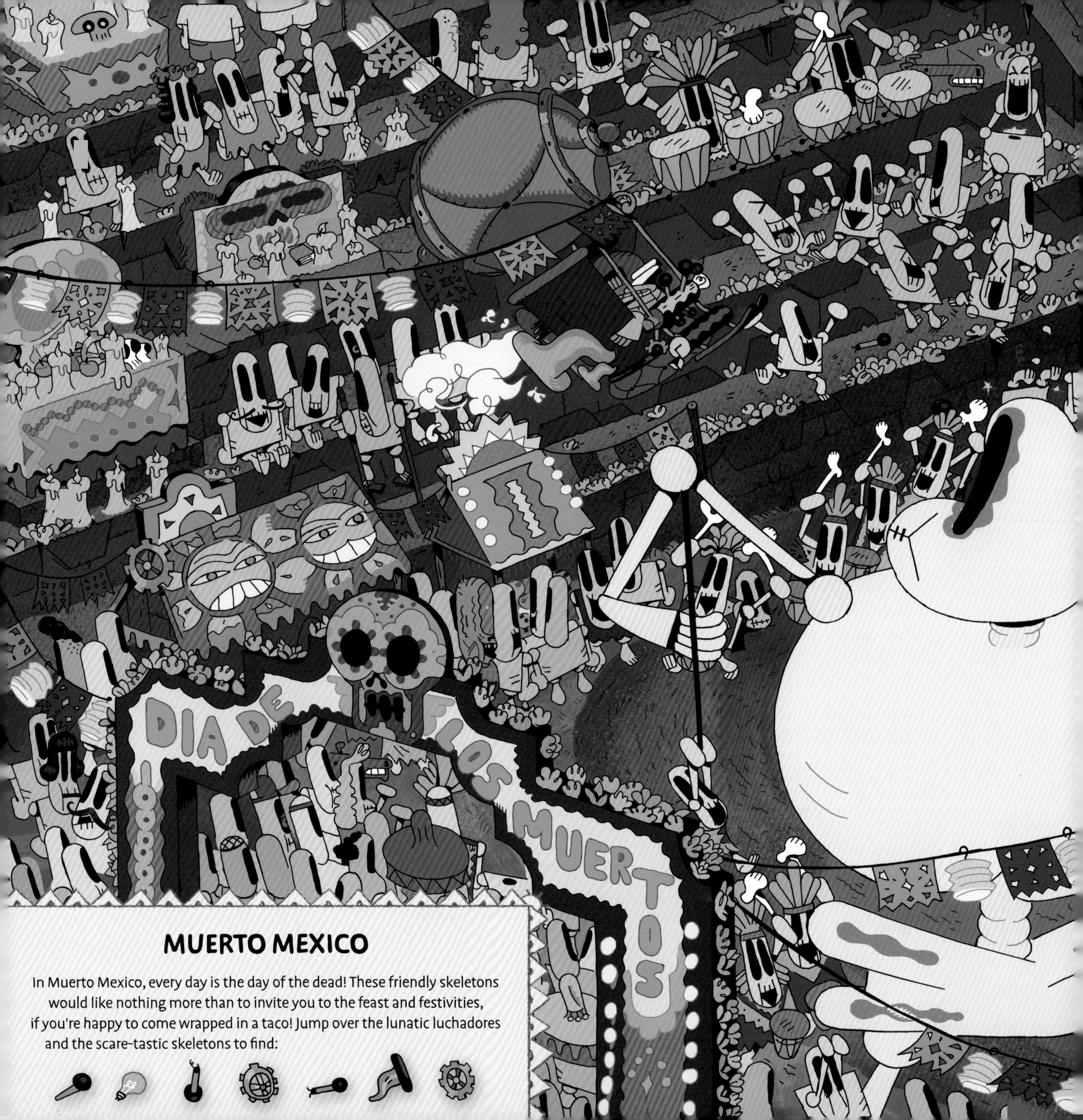
DIA DE LOS MUERTOS

MUERTO MEXICO

In Muerto Mexico, every day is the day of the dead! These friendly skeletons would like nothing more than to invite you to the feast and festivities, if you're happy to come wrapped in a taco! Jump over the lunatic luchadores and the scare-tastic skeletons to find:

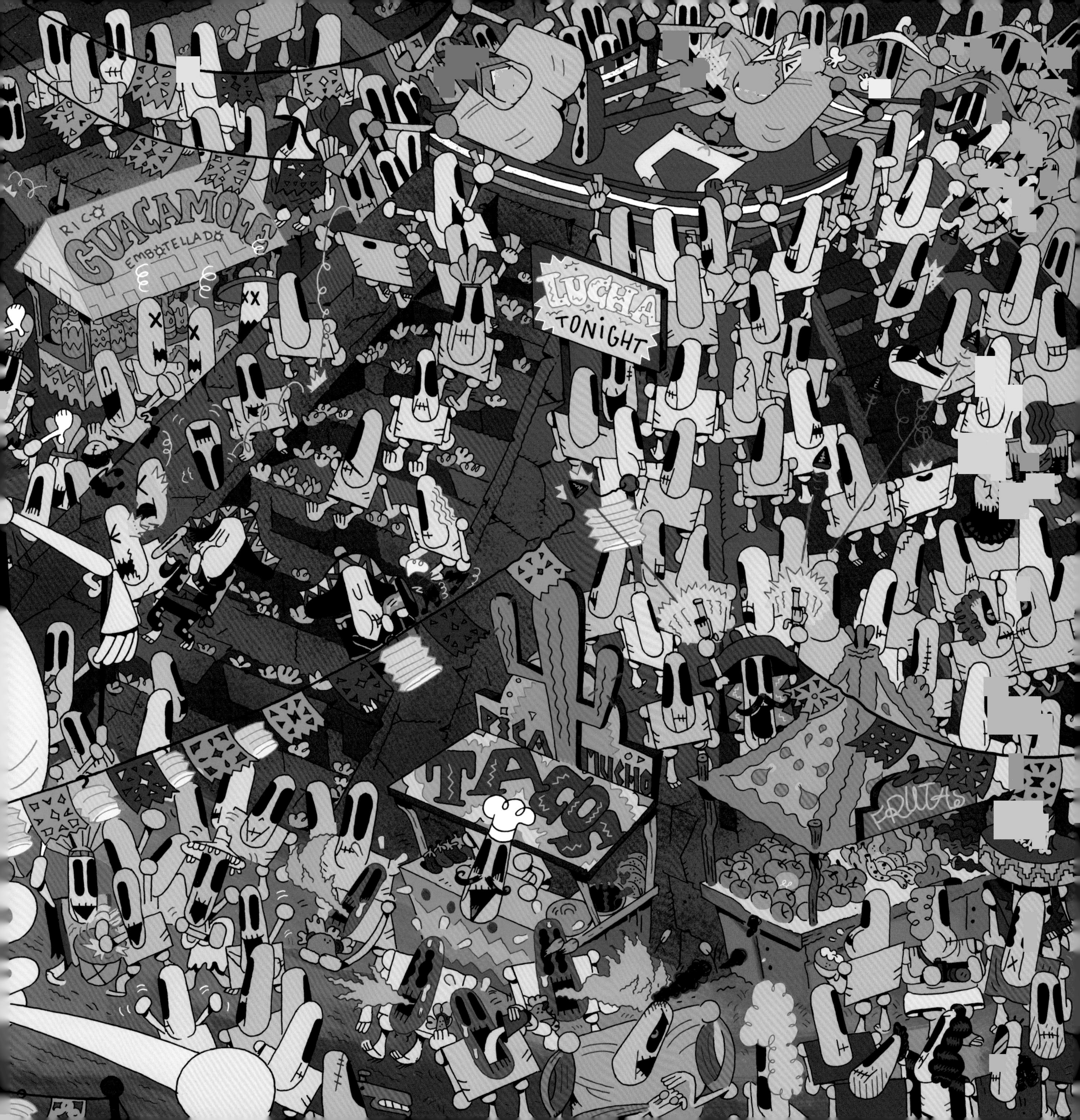
RICO GUACAMOLE EMBOTELLADO
LUCHA TONIGHT
PICA TACOS MUCHO
FRUTAS

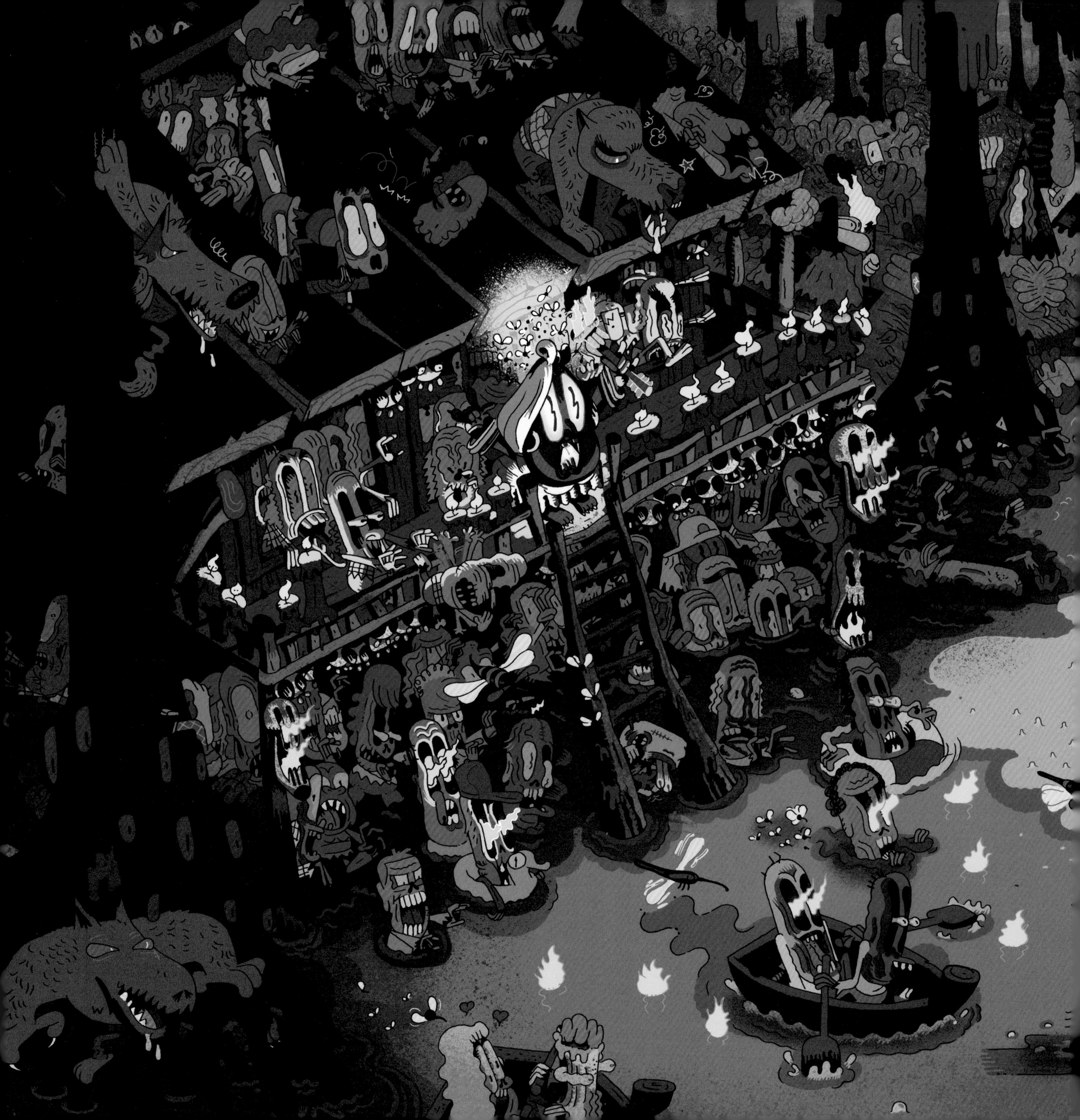

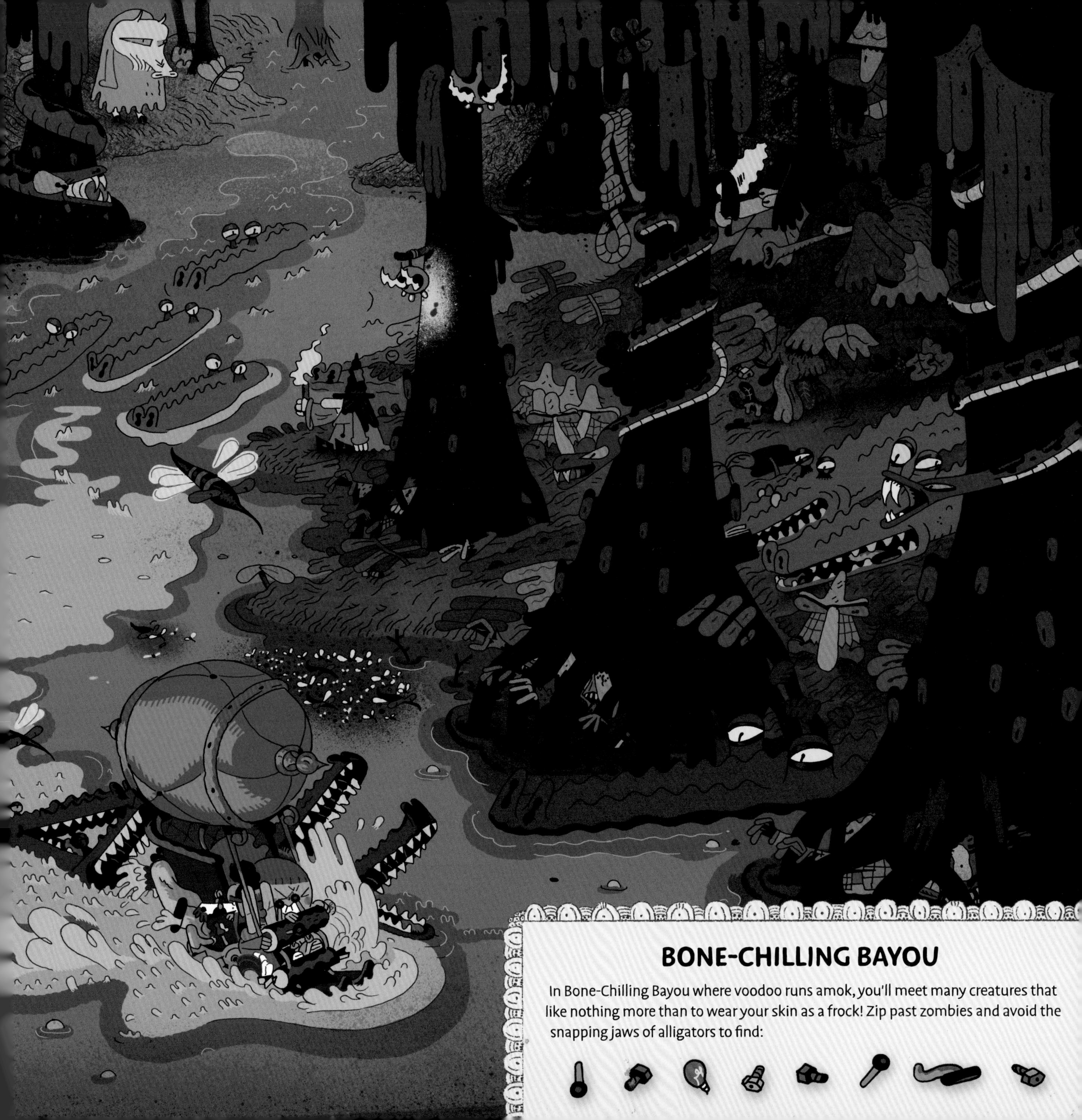

BONE-CHILLING BAYOU

In Bone-Chilling Bayou where voodoo runs amok, you'll meet many creatures that like nothing more than to wear your skin as a frock! Zip past zombies and avoid the snapping jaws of alligators to find:

HORRID HAWAII

Time for a break, this monster madness is getting tiresome! Relax on the beach in Hawaii, but here it's not just what lurks beneath the water that bites. As the drums of the tiki men get louder, you know you've got to move on... but first, you'll have to track down:

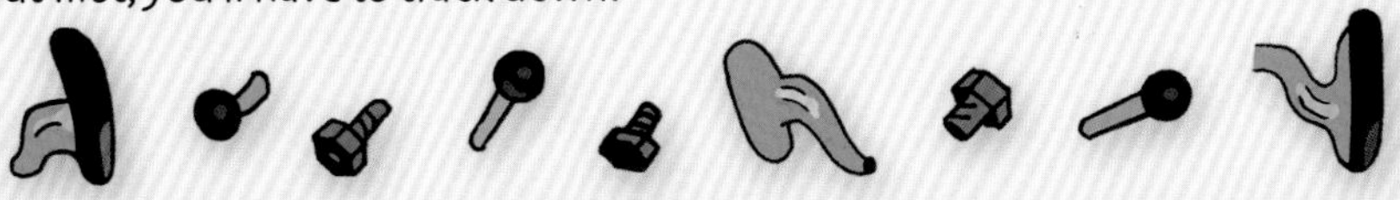

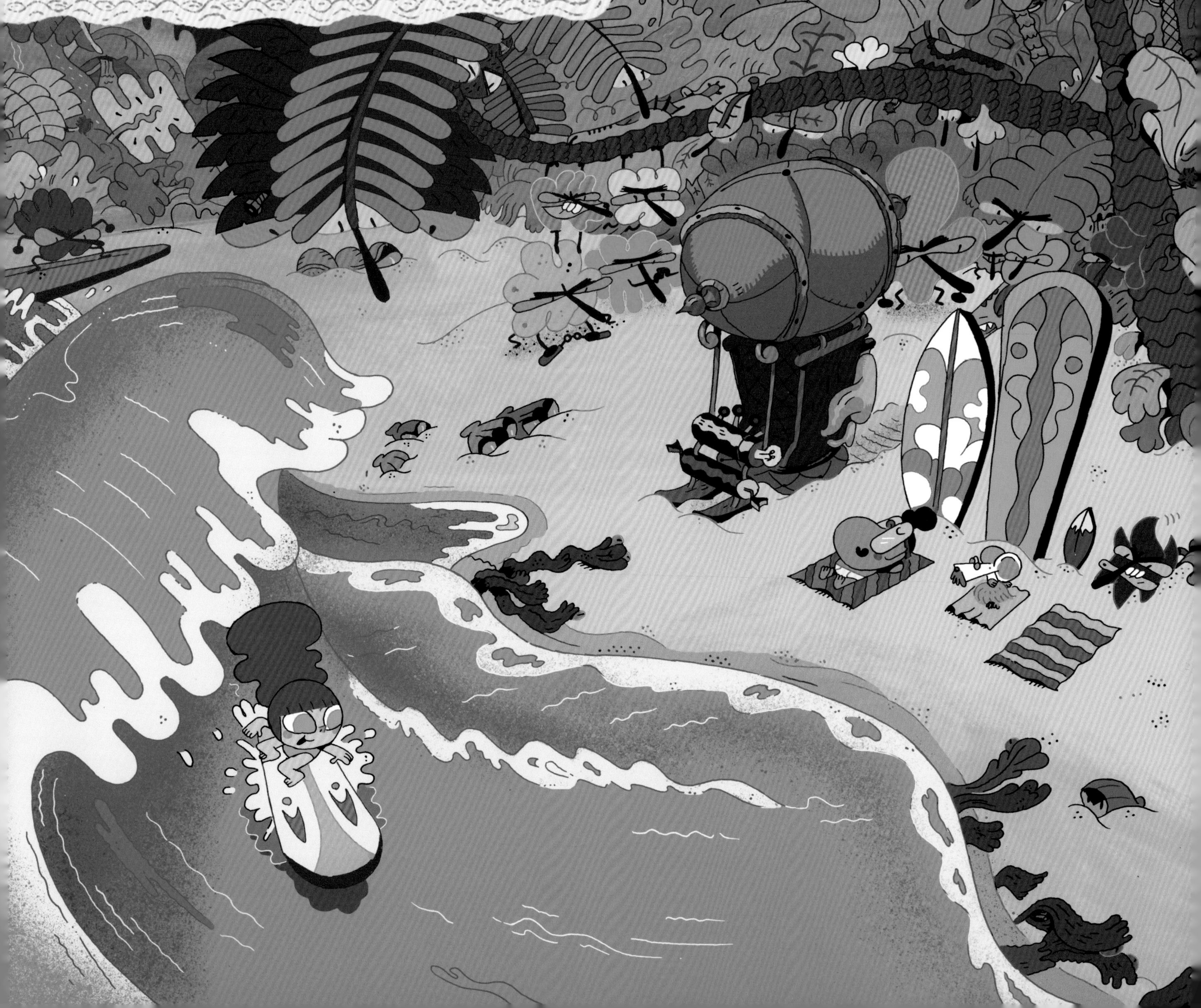

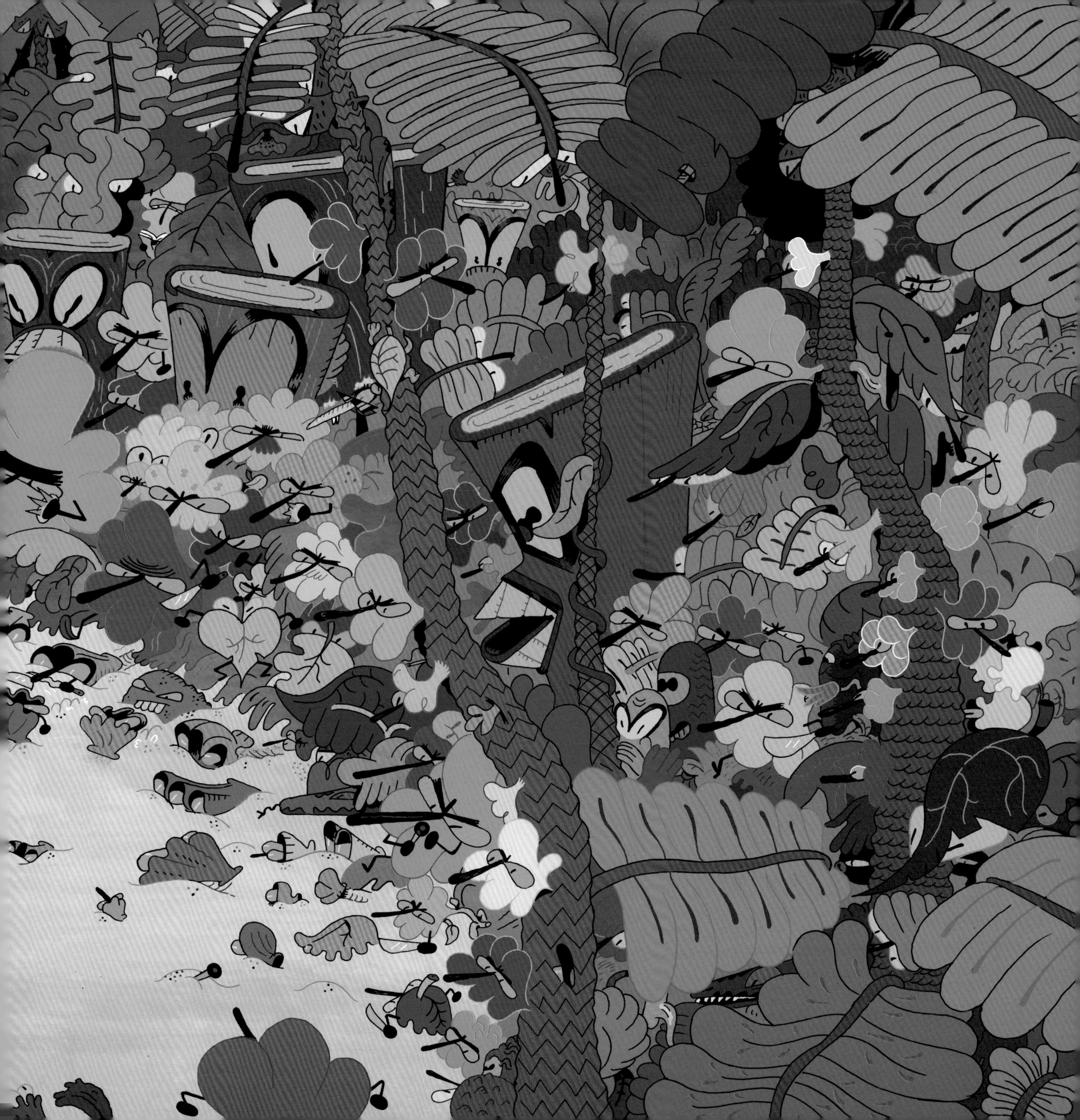

THE 'ORRIBLE OUTBACK

The outback can be a dangerous place, especially when the rocks have eyes... We're getting power back but you'll have to be quick and track:

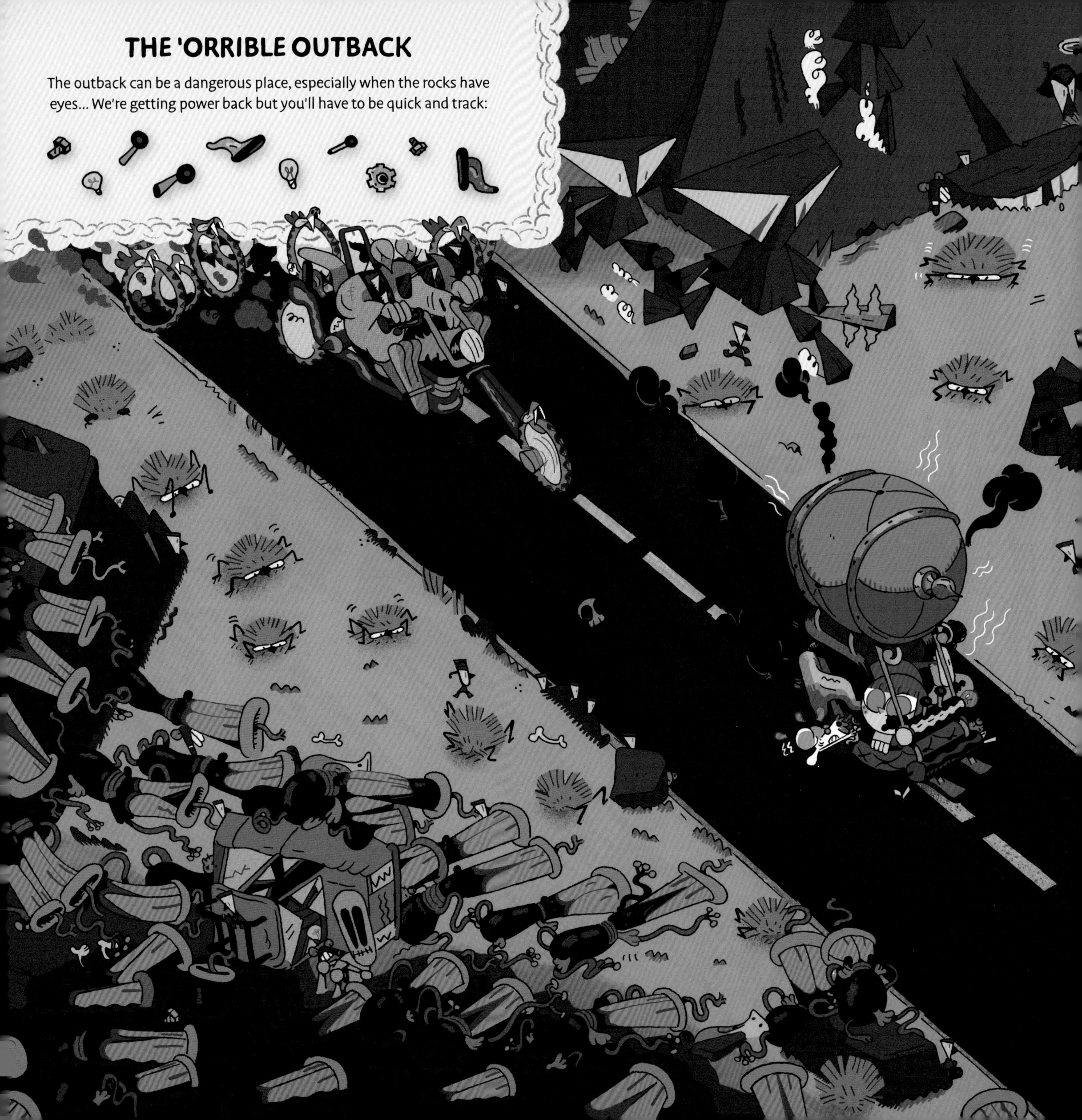

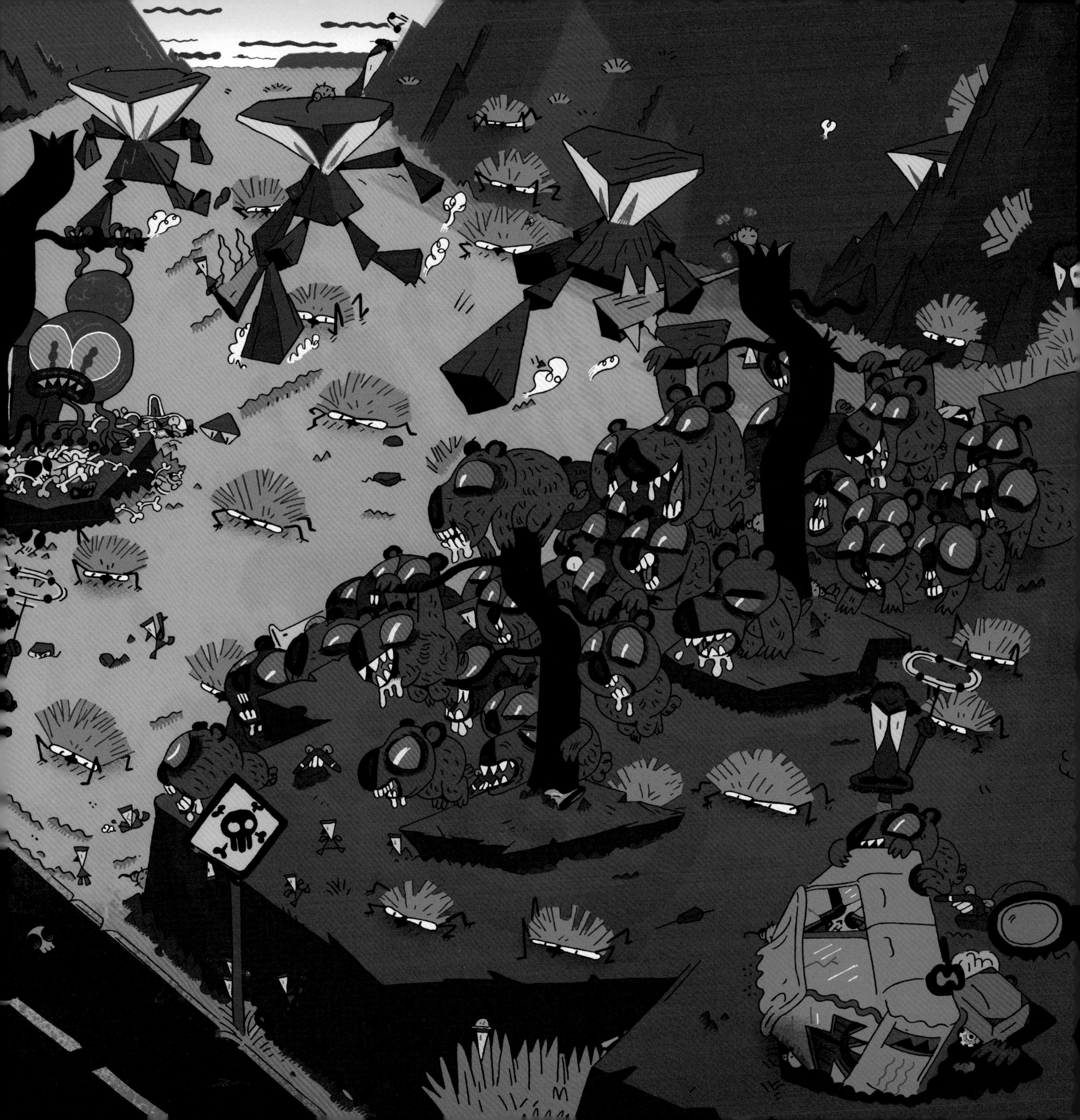

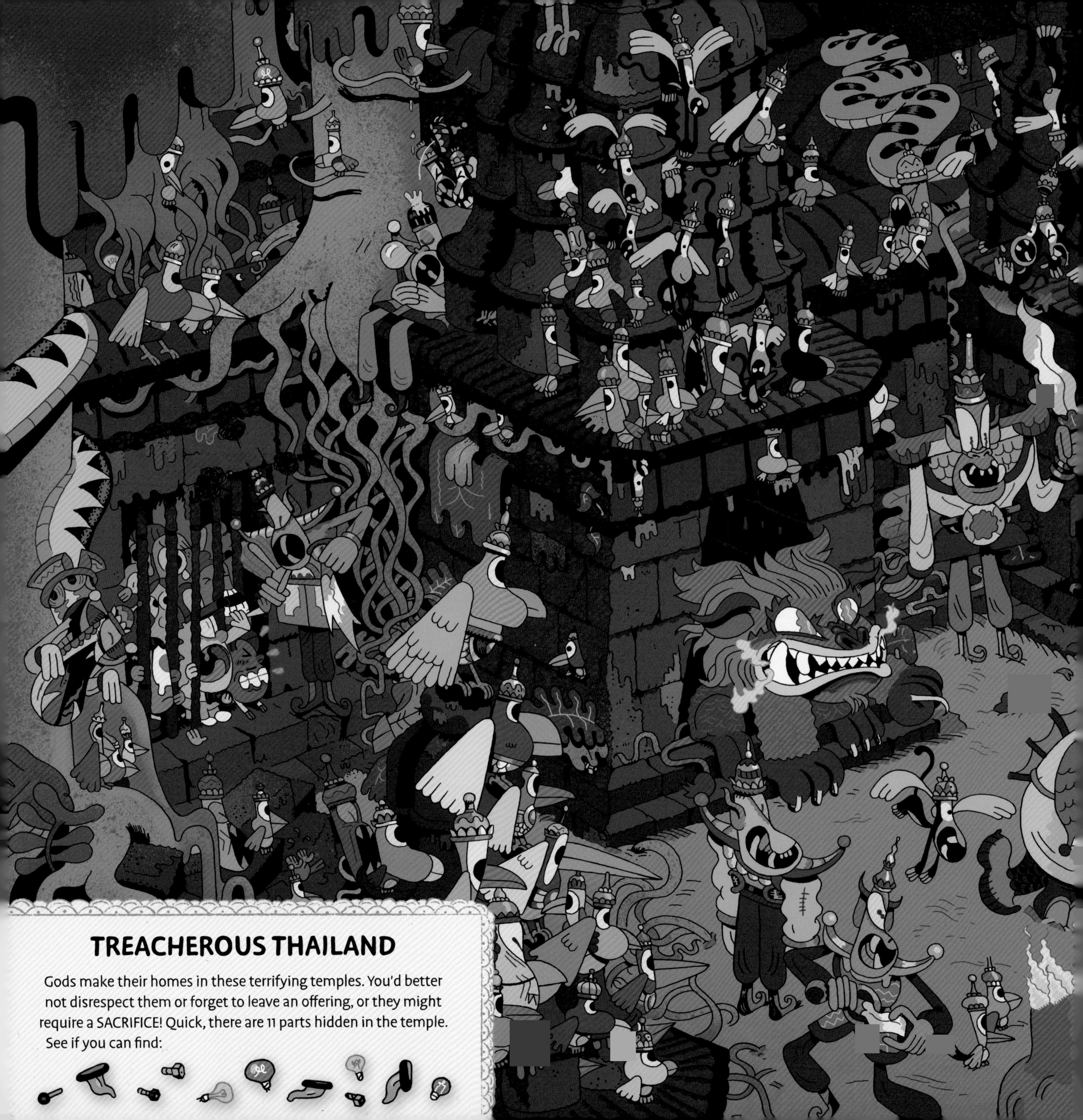

TREACHEROUS THAILAND

Gods make their homes in these terrifying temples. You'd better not disrespect them or forget to leave an offering, or they might require a SACRIFICE! Quick, there are 11 parts hidden in the temple. See if you can find:

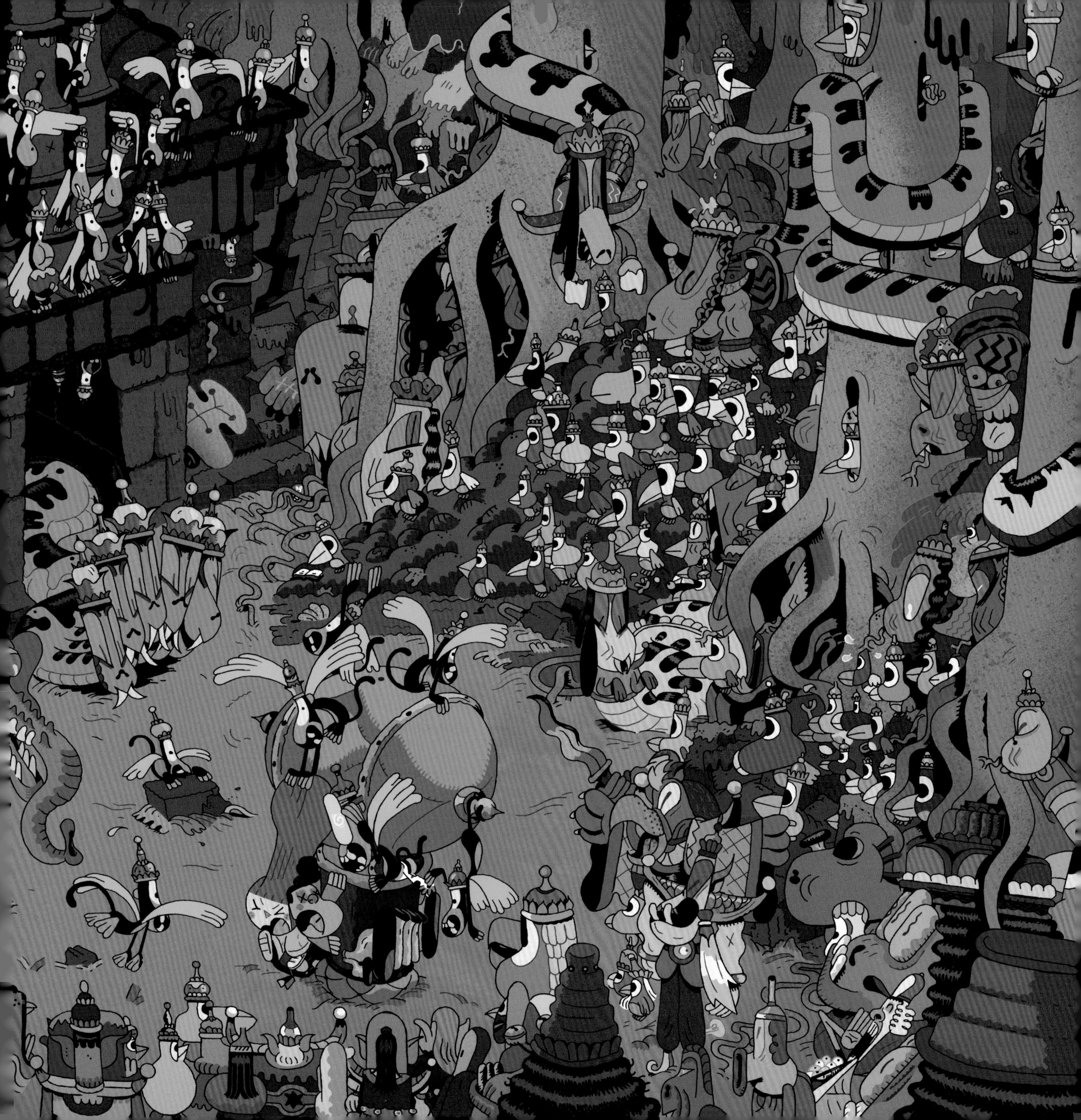

IMMORTAL INDIA

There's a battle raging between the monkey king and the demon army and I can see the last pieces of the puzzle and then we can go HOME! See if you can find them.

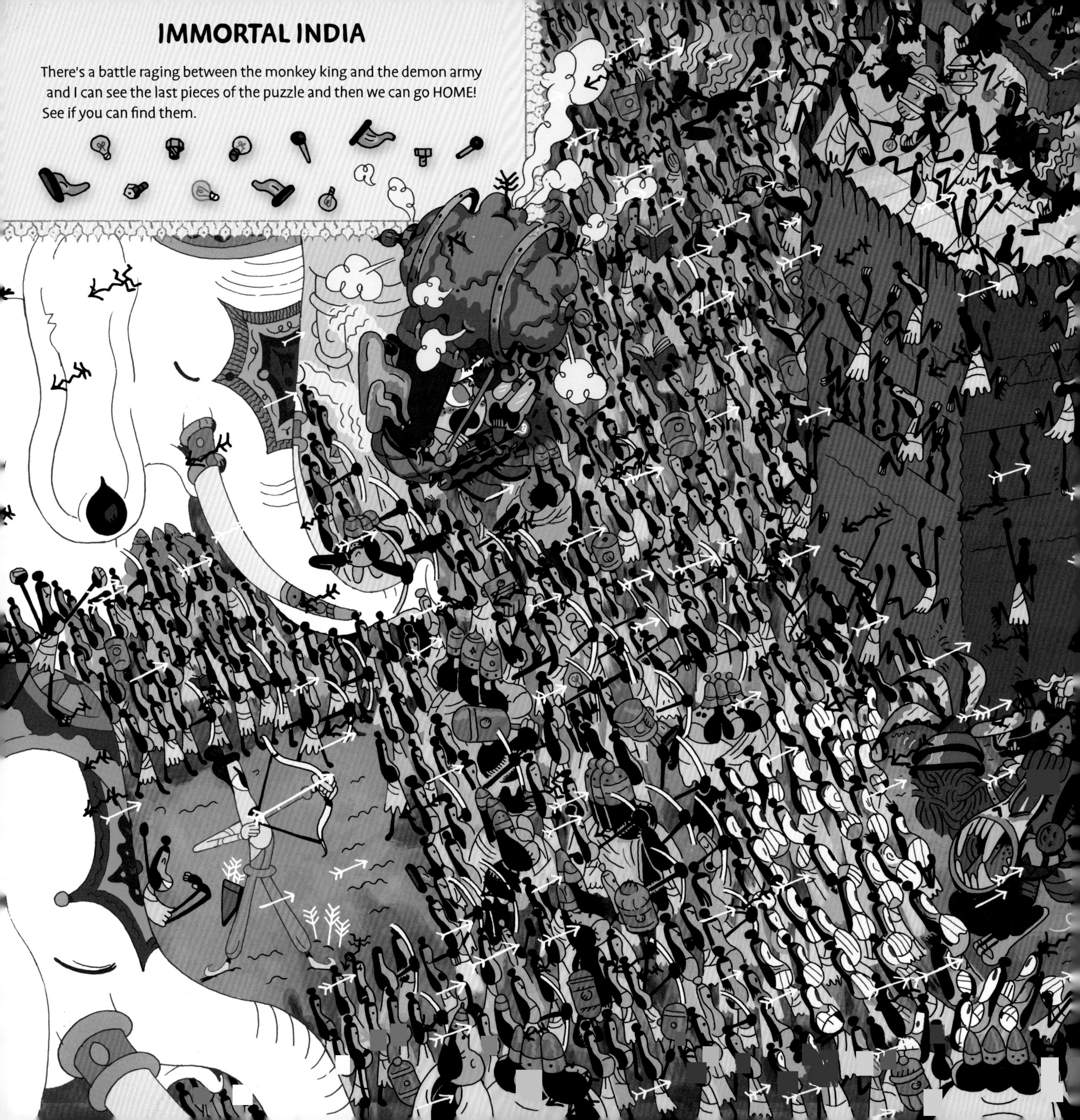

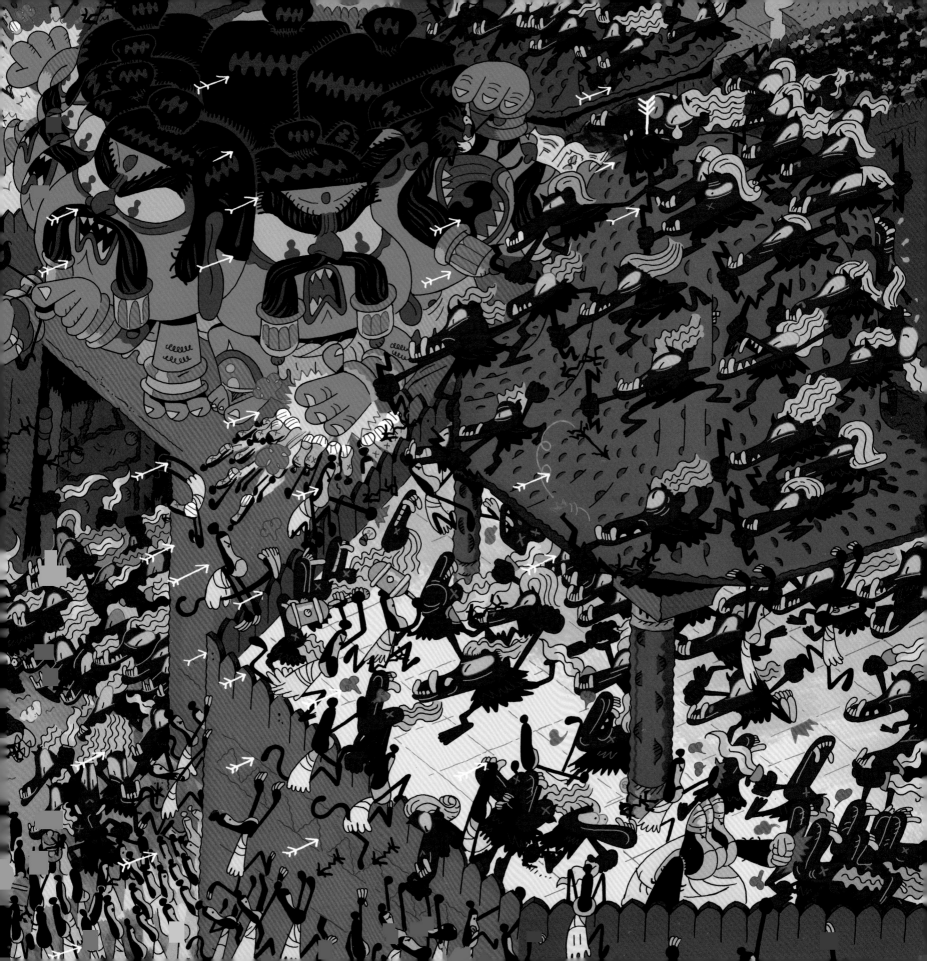

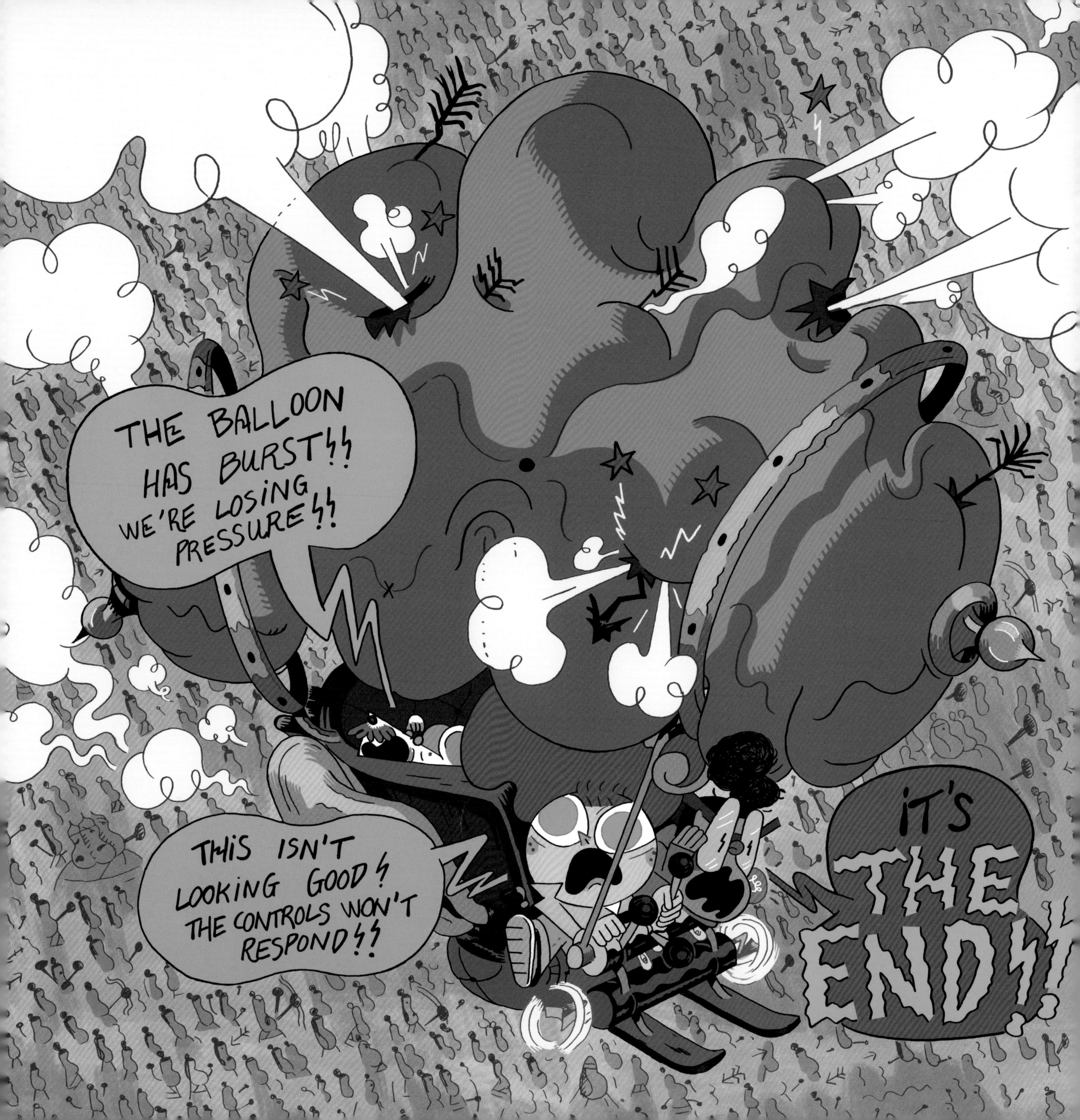
THE BALLOON HAS BURST!! WE'RE LOSING PRESSURE!!
THIS ISN'T LOOKING GOOD! THE CONTROLS WON'T RESPOND!!
IT'S THE END!!

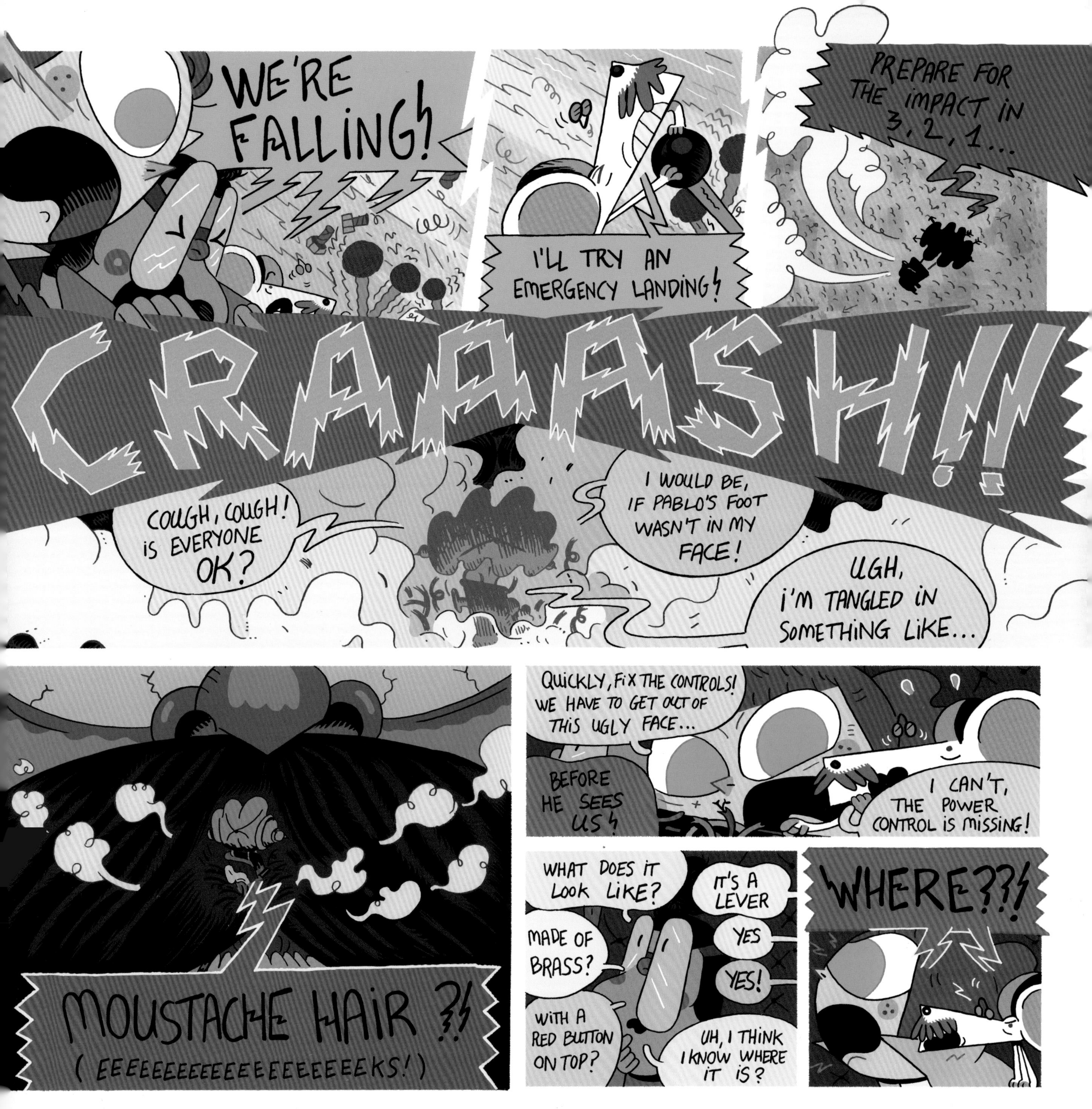
WE'RE FALLING!
I'LL TRY AN EMERGENCY LANDING!
PREPARE FOR THE IMPACT IN 3, 2, 1...
CRAAASH!!
COUGH, COUGH! IS EVERYONE OK?
I WOULD BE, IF PABLO'S FOOT WASN'T IN MY FACE!
UGH, I'M TANGLED IN SOMETHING LIKE...
MOUSTACHE HAIR ?!
(EEEEEEEEEEEEEEEEEEEEEKS!)
QUICKLY, FIX THE CONTROLS! WE HAVE TO GET OUT OF THIS UGLY FACE...
BEFORE HE SEES US!
I CAN'T, THE POWER CONTROL IS MISSING!
WHAT DOES IT LOOK LIKE?
IT'S A LEVER
MADE OF BRASS?
YES
YES!
WITH A RED BUTTON ON TOP?
UH, I THINK I KNOW WHERE IT IS?
WHERE??!

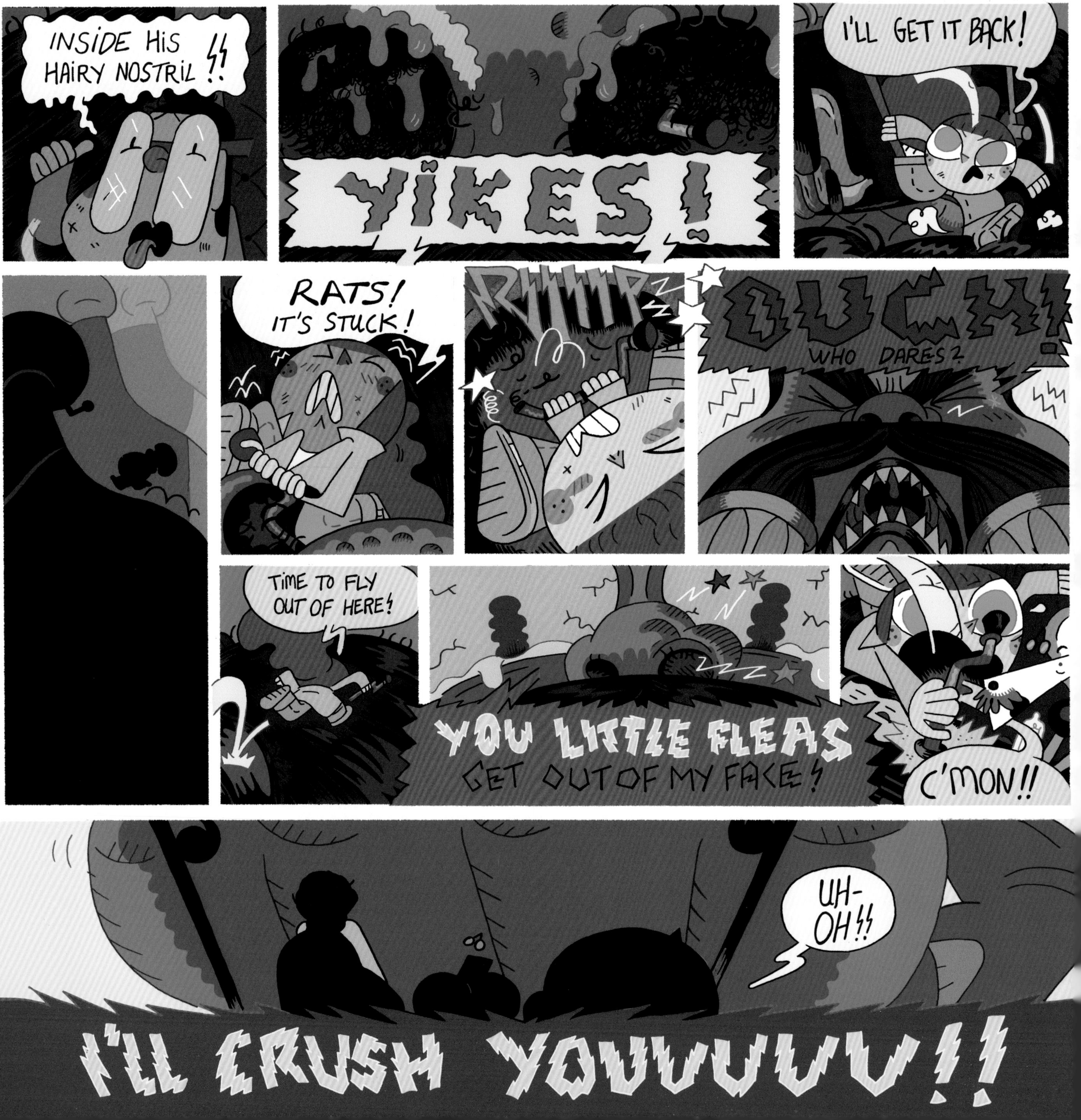
INSIDE HIS HAIRY NOSTRIL!!
YIKES!
I'LL GET IT BACK!
RATS! IT'S STUCK!
RHHHP
OUCH!
WHO DARES?
TIME TO FLY OUT OF HERE!
YOU LITTLE FLEAS
GET OUT OF MY FACE!
C'MON!!
UH-OH!!
I'LL CRUSH YOUUUUU!!

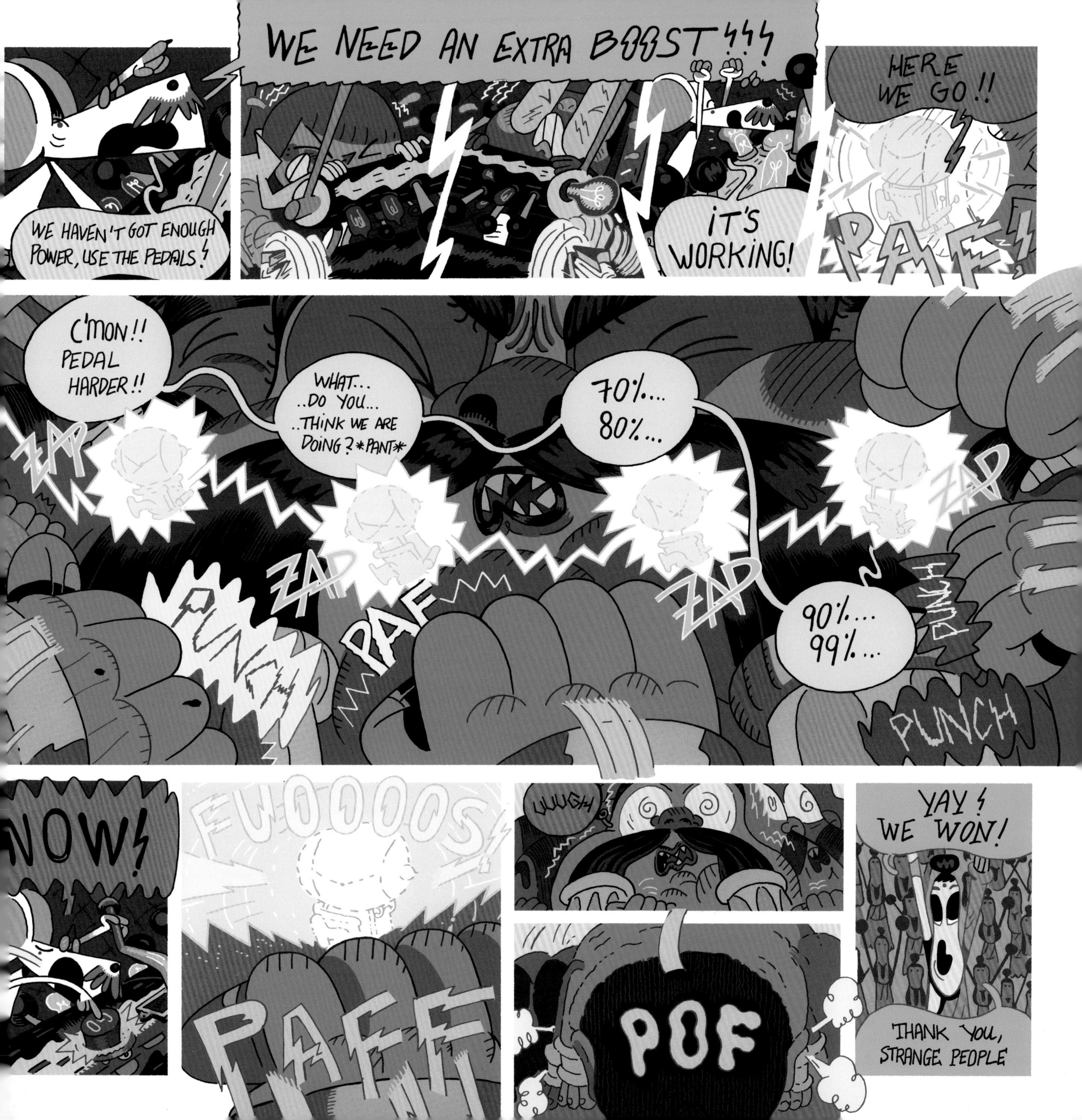
WE HAVEN'T GOT ENOUGH POWER, USE THE PEDALS!
WE NEED AN EXTRA BOOST!!!
IT'S WORKING!
HERE WE GO!!
PAF!
C'MON!! PEDAL HARDER!!
ZAP
WHAT... ..DO YOU... ..THINK WE ARE DOING? *PANT*
70%.... 80%....
ZAP
PUNCH
ZAP
PAF
ZAP
90%.... 99%....
PUNCH
PUNCH
NOW!
FUOOOOS!
PAFF
UUUGH
POF
YAY! WE WON!
THANK YOU, STRANGE PEOPLE

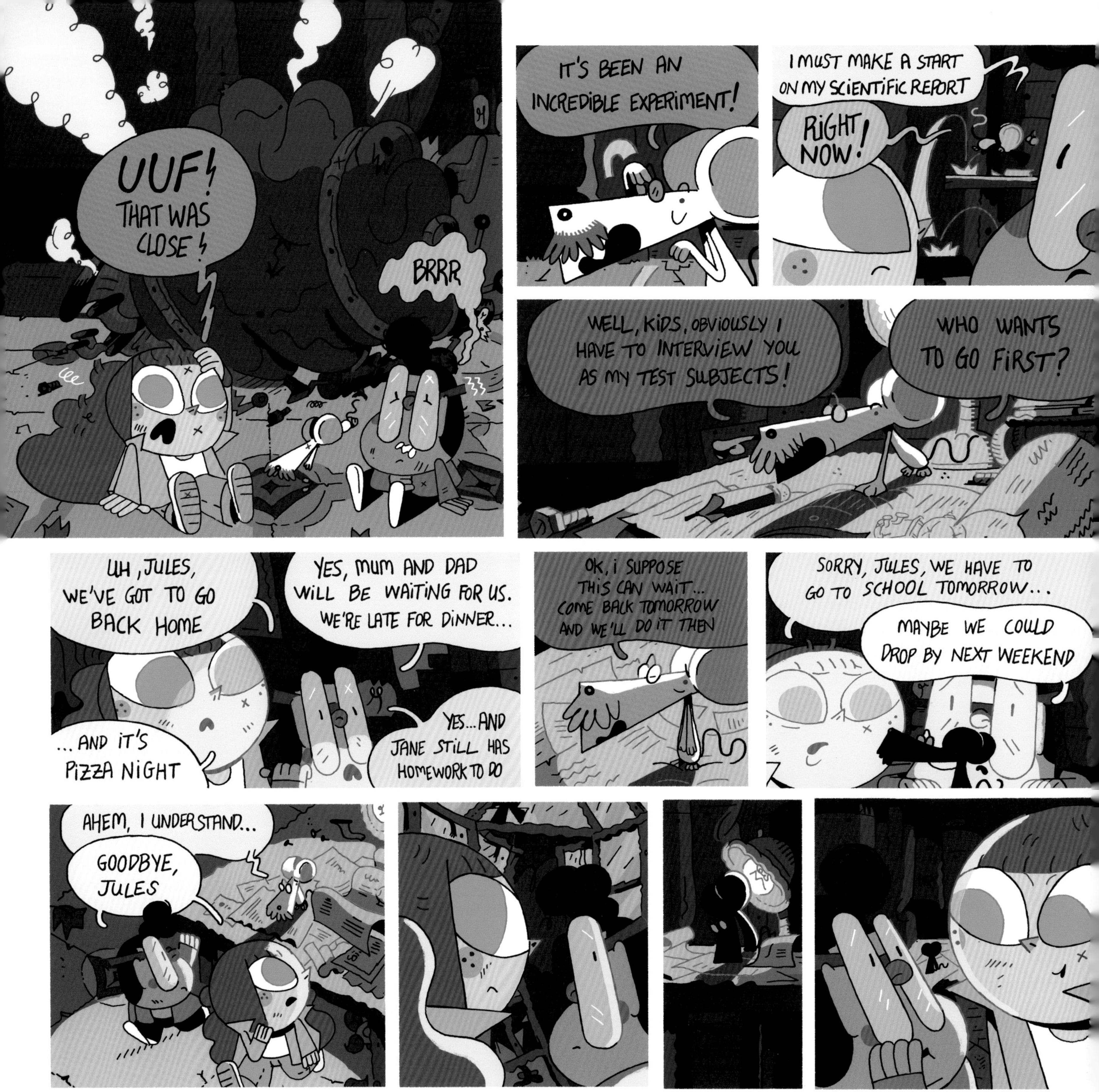
UUF! THAT WAS CLOSE!
BRRR
IT'S BEEN AN INCREDIBLE EXPERIMENT!
I MUST MAKE A START ON MY SCIENTIFIC REPORT
RIGHT NOW!
WELL, KIDS, OBVIOUSLY I HAVE TO INTERVIEW YOU AS MY TEST SUBJECTS!
WHO WANTS TO GO FIRST?
UH, JULES, WE'VE GOT TO GO BACK HOME
YES, MUM AND DAD WILL BE WAITING FOR US. WE'RE LATE FOR DINNER...
...AND IT'S PIZZA NIGHT
YES... AND JANE STILL HAS HOMEWORK TO DO
OK, I SUPPOSE THIS CAN WAIT... COME BACK TOMORROW AND WE'LL DO IT THEN
SORRY, JULES, WE HAVE TO GO TO SCHOOL TOMORROW...
MAYBE WE COULD DROP BY NEXT WEEKEND
AHEM, I UNDERSTAND...
GOODBYE, JULES

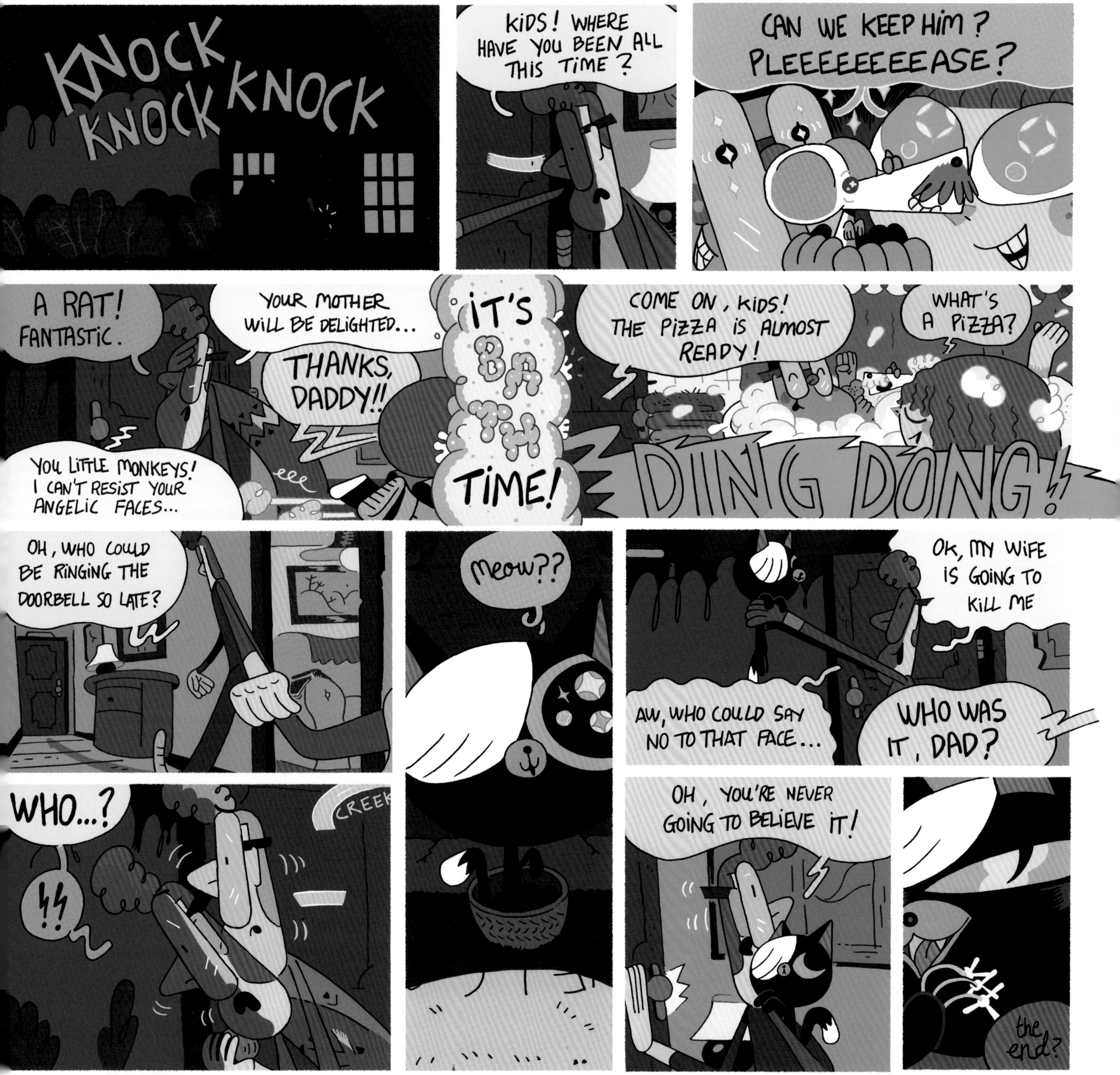

KNOCK KNOCK KNOCK
KIDS! WHERE HAVE YOU BEEN ALL THIS TIME?
CAN WE KEEP HIM? PLEEEEEEEEEASE?
A RAT! FANTASTIC.
YOUR MOTHER WILL BE DELIGHTED...
THANKS, DADDY!!
YOU LITTLE MONKEYS! I CAN'T RESIST YOUR ANGELIC FACES...
IT'S BATH TIME!
COME ON, KIDS! THE PIZZA IS ALMOST READY!
WHAT'S A PIZZA?
DING DONG!!
OH, WHO COULD BE RINGING THE DOORBELL SO LATE?
meow??
OK, MY WIFE IS GOING TO KILL ME
AW, WHO COULD SAY NO TO THAT FACE...
WHO WAS IT, DAD?
WHO...?
CREEK
OH, YOU'RE NEVER GOING TO BELIEVE IT!
the end?

Dr JULES' SCIENTIFIC

REPORT

Help Dr Jules complete his report by using your observational powers! Can you spot any of these things?

LOPSIDED LONDON

❑ Evil flower from Horrid Hawaii
❑ The ghosts of Sir Francis Bacon and the Frozen Chicken
❑ King Henry VIII going for a walk with his wives and dogs
❑ Monster doing the washing up (and annoyed by it)
❑ Phantom Sherlock Holmes & Dr Watson
❑ A goblin robbing a head
❑ Someone sleeping

NOCTURNAL NORWAY

❑ Demon from Immortal India
❑ A human running away
❑ A troll reading
❑ Elvis Trollsley
❑ A troll acquiring a house
❑ A blonde troll
❑ A handsome troll (compared to the others, that is)

TERRIFYING TRANSYLVANIA

❑ Monkey from Treacherous Thailand
❑ 2 vampire cooks
❑ Werewolf carrying a skull
❑ A vampire reading
❑ A sneaky vampire hunter hiding
❑ 11 werewolves
❑ A group of humans who thought they'd escaped

MONSTROUS MOSCOW

❑ Strange creature from the 'Orrible Outback
❑ 2 frogs
❑ There are 5 types of dragons: green, yellow, red, purple and blue. Can you see them all?
❑ A fish with one eye
❑ A dwarf having a sandwich
❑ A dwarf fishing
❑ A dwarf ice skating

AGELESS ATHENS

❑ Dwarf from Monstrous Moscow
❑ 7 snack vendors
❑ The 3 old hags who cut the thread of life
❑ The thread of life about to cause an accident
❑ 4 Medusas
❑ A spectator being suffocated by a snake
❑ Spectators using a cell phone

MACABRE MARRAKECH

❑ Skeleton from Mexico
❑ 12 bouncy eyes that escaped from the food shop!
❑ Find Dr Jules!
❑ Find a way for Dr Jules to return to the Hot Air Contraption!
❑ Find the 2 halves of the half-man
❑ Find the 4 runaway genies
❑ A very stinky shop
❑ A musician

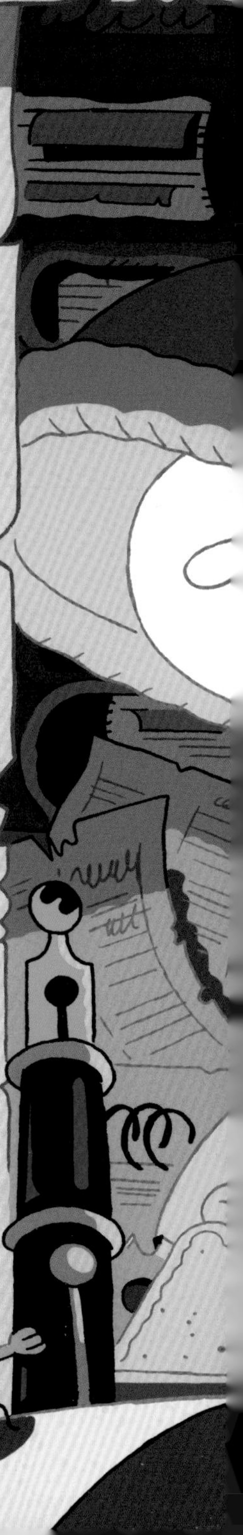

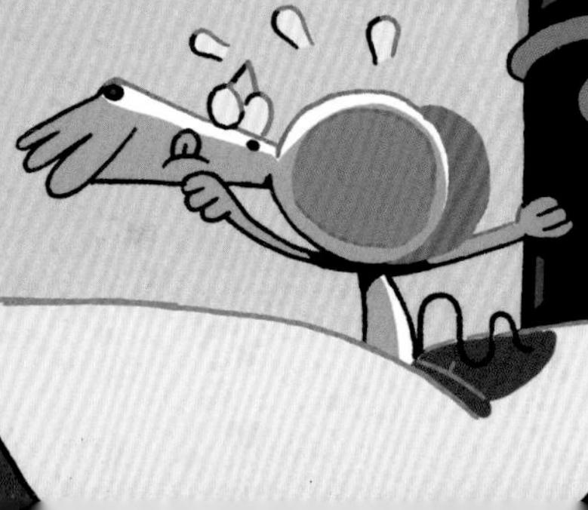

MUERTO MEXICO

- ❏ Zombie from Bone-chilling Bayou
- ❏ 6 skeletons with moustaches
- ❏ Someone taking a nap
- ❏ 3 strange orange dogs
- ❏ A body without a head
- ❏ 2 heads rolling down
- ❏ A skeleton on stilts

BONE-CHILLING BAYOU

- ❏ Troll from Nocturnal Norway
- ❏ 5 witches
- ❏ 3 skulls with eyes
- ❏ 2 zombies in love
- ❏ 2 zombies in rubber rings who can't swim
- ❏ 4 werewolves
- ❏ 2 zombies wearing baseball caps

HORRID HAWAII

- ❏ Vampire from Terrifying Transylvania
- ❏ 6 red dandelions
- ❏ 12 mad coconuts
- ❏ Have you seen the flower with a moustache?
- ❏ And the reading flower?
- ❏ 8 lizards
- ❏ A surfing flower

'ORRIBLE OUTBACK

- ❏ Half-man from Macabre Marrakech
- ❏ 3 platypuses
- ❏ A koala bear who wears glasses
- ❏ And 2 drivers who never made it
- ❏ 5 men with lassoes
- ❏ 6 angry boomerangs
- ❏ 12 ferocious kiwi birds

TREACHEROUS THAILAND

- ❏ Snack vendor from Ageless Athens
- ❏ 2 monkeys eating fruit
- ❏ 2 monkeys playing a prank on a guard
- ❏ Someone reading
- ❏ A very big snake
- ❏ 2 guards sleeping
- ❏ And some humans being told off

IMMORTAL INDIA

- ❏ Boggart from Lopsided London
- ❏ Some monkey men reading
- ❏ Some monkey men napping
- ❏ The arrow that backfired
- ❏ Have you seen the well-groomed demons?
- ❏ And 13 three-headed monkeys!

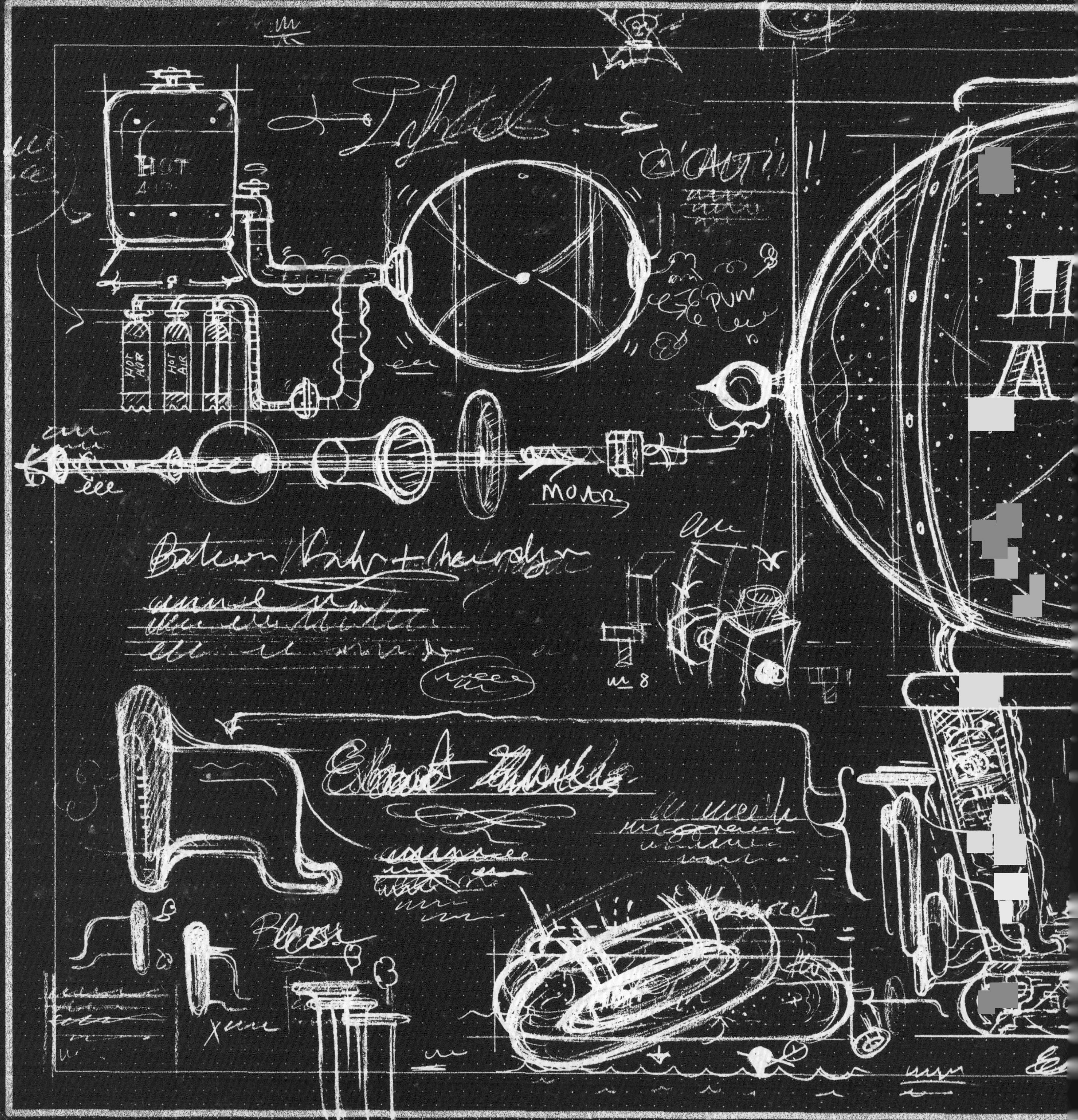

HOT
HOT AIR
HOT AIR
MOTOR